Falling
for
Mr. Sometimes

(book four of the Falling for Mr. Wrong series)

by Jenny Gardiner

Copyright © 2018 by Jenny Gardiner
Cover art by Kim Killion, The Killion Group, Inc.
ISBN-13: 978-1-944763-19-0

Author's Note

You guys! I have to tell you, this book realllllly didn't want to be written!

It was the first book ever I was scheduled to get done a month early (I'm a deadliner so I never finish early)! I was so excited about this. I'm always at the wire and my editor (shout-out to the awesome Nikki Busch) is usually giving me a mulligan of a couple of days to turn it in.

But this time I was going to Australia—for our daughter's engagement party!—so I was planning to be free and clear of deadlines so that I didn't have the book looming over me while gone.

Ahhh…but that's when the darned flu came knockin' on my door (more like sledgehammered the door in). Which ended up not officially being the flu after all, but was for all intents and purposes just like it. So I got sick as a dog the week before we left, which meant there was no writing going on.

I remained feeling a bit under the weather while in Australia though toughed it out so we could enjoy ourselves (had a great time), but never had a moment to write. I returned home with bronchitis and a sinus infection, still feeling not so great, and no book finished. Kind Nikki gave me some leeway to get it written while I got to the doctor to get some more medicine to help heal me, and then ugh, Easter morning I woke up with the worst stomachache!

But it turns out it wasn't my stomach, and for a good day and a half I was doubled over in pain, dying—I was convinced I was! And I probably could have, had they not finally diagnosed me with acute appendicitis.

On the first day of the gut pain I actually wrote—I dutifully parked my butt on the sofa and wrote through the pain for the entire afternoon. The second day I optimistically brought my laptop to bed with me after my first visit to the doctor but that was just wishful thinking—instead I lay in my bed drifting in and out of consciousness till, in desperation, we went back to the doctor, and then on to the ER (where my daughter was working, yay, but where they don't move you to the front of the line just because you have a relative working there, waaaa!) We got to the ER around 4:45 p.m. and didn't get a bed in the ER till about 9:00 p.m.; and it wasn't till 3

What people are saying about Jenny Gardiner's books:

Red Hot Romeo

"Awesome". So enjoyed the romantic chemistry between the two characters. Read it non stop into the wee hours. Highly recommend this book
-- Mrs. K

Blue-Blooded Romeo

"Another brilliant, fun read from Jenny Gardiner. The book is fun to read and I thoroughly enjoyed every word. Jenny Gardiner has put the fun back into romance books and I look forward to each book in this delightful series."
-- Anne Blyth

"I had planned on only reading a few chapters at first but couldn't put it down. A terrific storyline, well-developed and extremely relatable characters, what's not to love?? Great read!"
-- Samantha Reeves

Big O Romeo

"I could not put this book down. Warning don't start this book late at night as you will not want to stop reading.
    -- Di

Sleeping with Ward Cleaver

"A fun, sassy read! A cross between Erma Bombeck and Candace Bushnell, reading Jenny Gardiner is like sinking your teeth into a chocolate cupcake...you just want more."
    --Meg Cabot, NY Times bestselling author of Princess Diaries, Queen of Babble and more

Slim to None

"Jenny Gardiner has done it again--this fun, fast-paced book is a great summer read."
    --Sarah Pekkanen, NY Times bestselling author of *The Opposite of Me*

a.m. that they finally wheeled me into the operating room. My poor husband had just returned from Australia Easter night (he'd stayed on to hike for four days in Tasmania) and was super jet-lagged and even tried to grab some sleep on the ER floor—hardly where one wants to sleep, right?!).

I ended up having emergency surgery and yeah, that then set me back even more as far as getting my book written. So a few weeks late I finally turned this darned book over to Nikki, and I hope you can't tell what stages during this book I was just miserable with viruses and a rogue appendix! I have faith that Nikki will polish it all up so you'll be none the wiser!

And I'm super grateful to Nikki and my formatter, the fabulous Joanne Levy, who both squeezed me in late due to my unfortunate medical issues. And enormous thanks to my sleep-deprived husband Scott and my daughter Gillian who pulled an all-nighter with us at the hospital after already working a day shift. I don't think I could have survived without their amazing help and support!

Here's hoping that is all behind me now and I can finish the final book in this series—Falling for Mr. Right—early. And then I've got another series I'm noodling—more about that when Mr. Right is released.

In the meantime, thanks for reading Mr. Sometimes and hope you enjoy it!

-·|·-

```
  ..· ''"")) -·|·-
 ,·´ ·´'"")).·´'"")) -·|·- ·´
((,.·´ ..·´Jenny-·|·-
·|·- ((,.·´'* -·|·- ´* -·|·- ´*
```

-·|·-

Chapter One

SO maybe Jamie Lundquist had grown a little plump lately, although she preferred the term "fluffy." It was a woman's prerogative, right? Especially after all of that holiday celebrating she'd suffered through recently. A little Christmas party appetizer here, a little (all right, let's be honest: a *lot*) of New Year's Eve drinking there, and the next thing you know, your ass is dragging, your clothes have morphed from merely snug to oh-crap-the-zipper-of-your-jeans-won't-go-up, and you long for the days when you could pinch just an inch. Nothing a little effort at the gym (not to mention some self-restraint at mealtime) couldn't fix, right?

That's why she found herself slogging off to Verity Beach's one-and-only fitness center on a frigid January morning against her better judgment. If that wasn't bad enough, an early morning workout flew in the face of her normal wintertime sleep pattern, submerged beneath the cozy comfort of a goose down duvet till nine. It wasn't even dawn when she arrived at the place, knowing it would be yet another day of parking space roulette. In January, it seemed the amateurs—like her—came out to the gym in droves, and parking was at an all-time premium. God forbid she parked a block away and walked the extra few hundred feet. No way, man! It was freezing, and she was already going to have to exert herself far more than usual in the dead of winter once she got inside. She had to preserve her energy stores!

So she did what she'd done every day since returning to the scene of her now-daily penance, driving sloth-slow, scouring the horizon in the hopes that someone would be pulling out and she could nab the space. She glanced at the far corner of the ample parking lot and spied what appeared to be a spot, flooring it to get there before anyone else did. But once she approached, she realized that for the third time this week, some yahoo with a fancy vehicle—this time a sleek, shiny, new black SUV—had taken it upon himself (the people who did this sort of thing were always men) to straddle two spaces to protect his car from door dings.

Dammit. This sort of thing chapped Jamie's burgeoning ass big-time. Didn't the moron know that January at the gym was parking lot purgatory? In the post-holiday competition to undo what the season of joy had wrought, it seemed all that good cheer was being diminished by selfish bastards like this guy, who couldn't simply take a space and hope for the best with his precious car.

Well, she would show him. She sized up the remaining half-space, confident that if she couldn't fit her fat butt into her jeans, at least she could wedge her modestly sized car into this demi-space. Thank goodness vehicles didn't gain weight with too much celebrating. She glanced in her mirror, pulled forward, then put the gear shift in reverse, checking the backup camera on her dashboard, ever-so-gingerly drifting backward as she masterfully squeezed into the remaining void.

Jamie couldn't help but feel a bit smug about her accomplishment, even though it meant the jerk would not be able to get back into his car on the driver's side.

"Oh well. That's his problem," she muttered as she put the car in park. "Let him climb in with all the spare room he has on the passenger side."

But as she checked and rechecked her positioning, she started to feel a teensy bit guilty and took a couple more passes to straighten out her car. She even made sure her tires hugged the curb on the other side of the space to allow as much room as possible for Mr. Selfish to maybe—if he lost weight after his holiday bingeing—get into his pretentious penis-substitute-on-wheels through the driver's side door.

She turned off the ignition, exited onto the curb, and dusted off her hands, mission accomplished. She'd practically had her exercise for the day and even entertained the idea that she could shorten her workout after this arduous parking job. But no: she was here, surfing season would soon be upon her, and she wasn't going to move up a size in a wet suit because she took her holiday celebrating—and her parents' contentious divorce—too seriously. She was gonna wrangle that same discipline that led her to rise before dawn to surf each morning, once the weather was not so hostile, and SoulCycle her ass down to a more manageable size.

As she fumbled in her purse for her gym pass next to the manly-man SUV, she was bowled over by the noxious fumes from what must have been a skunk or something. Yuck. The guy probably ran it over for sport. Bad enough she had to park near this jerk, but for the air around her car to be enveloped in the nasty fug of skunk aroma, well, ugh. For good measure, she decided to slip a note onto this bonehead's windshield, letting him know, in case he was unaware, that his parking job was lame. She rifled through her purse and pulled out a notebook and pen, pulling the cap off with her teeth. She leaned against the hood of her car as she scrawled out her message, lifted one of the car's windshield wipers and secured the note beneath it, then headed into the fitness center.

After starting the day on a sour note, she was feeling good about herself, her determination, and her destiny to return to fit and petite, ASAP.

It was gonna be a great day.

Chapter Two

CARTER Henderson's day seemed to go from bad to worse. And dawn was barely breaking. This didn't bode well. First he had to wake up the neighbor he barely knew to help him jump-start the battery on his "new" used SUV, the one he'd saved up for over a year to buy. He was bummed that he already had a problem with it, since the acquisition of this vehicle was the closest he'd come to commitment in, well, ever.

Sure, he'd toughed it out through some unpleasant obligations in life already: like living through the shitshow that had been his parents' dismal marriage for half his childhood. And yeah, even though he'd realized midway through college that the accounting degree he was working toward would lead to a career that was not what he wanted to do for the rest of his days on earth, he sucked it up and graduated, despite wishing he'd gone to culinary school instead.

But now that wasn't in his meager budget, especially with paying off student loans and constantly bailing his irresponsible father out of financial jams. Instead he'd taken side jobs doing the books for a number of small businesses while working crazy hours as a sous chef at a variety of restaurants all over the Outer Banks, learning on the job how to be the best chef he could be, minus the formal training.

So even though he was tired as shit, he dragged himself out of bed in the pitch dark of a cold January morning to keep his commitment to himself to pursue self-care. Working his crazy hours meant if he wasn't careful, he'd end up a paunchy, sweaty, miserable, beer-bellied crank like so many chefs he'd encountered along the way. He wasn't going to be that guy.

But damn, taking care of yourself sometimes translated into kicking said self to the curb. Certainly on days like today. It didn't help that on his way to the gym this morning, he'd run over a skunk. He'd swerved to miss the thing but a few more inches and he'd have plowed into oncoming traffic, which would have made it a much worse day. But he felt awful about killing the poor skunk, who'd done nothing wrong.

Once he got to the gym, he vowed things would improve, pronto. Instead, he wrenched his ankle while on the treadmill, then some dumbbell actually dropped a dumbbell on his hand when he was on the ground stretching. Luckily it was a senior citizen, and the weight was one of those that was so light you wondered why anyone even bothered to use it for resistance. He learned the hard way that it might be light, but not when it lands on a delicate body part. So yeah, this day had not gotten off to a great start.

To top it off, as he limped toward his SUV, he saw that some jerk had wedged their crap car into that space that was left after he had to straddle two spaces when he'd arrived. Annoyingly, when he'd gotten to the gym, someone next to him had overstepped the parking lines by a good two feet, so he had to do the same thing. Now he wouldn't be able to get into his damned truck, made all the worse because of his new ankle injury.

He eyeballed how the hell he was going to flatten himself like a field mouse trying to squeeze into a hole in a house. No way was he going to be able to enter through the driver's side; he'd have to be as thin as a sheet of paper to fit there. Not to mention he'd hate to ding the person's car doors, even if the guy (because it was always a guy who did those things) was a jerk for parking there.

He assessed the passenger side, realizing there was no way in hell he could enter there either—the car next to him was parked in such a cockeyed way that he was stuck until the owners of those cars came out.

He cupped his hands and blew into them, failing to warm himself against the bitter cold, trying to figure out why he thought a beach town would always be temperate because it's at the beach. Totally blond mistake. Well, he was paying for that oversight now as he paced back and forth behind the SUV in his gym shorts, wishing he had coffee, or even hot water, to warm him up. To make matters worse, he'd planned to run to and from the car and hadn't brought sweatpants along. Yet another blond mistake. He was piling them up this morning.

He glanced over to the little Mazda two-door that had jammed in next to him and noticed the cool glow of an iPhone light in the interior of the car. Well, hell— someone must've been in there all along. He raced over to the driver's side door and pounded on the window.

In the dim predawn light, a pretty face turned and its owner stared at him, but she didn't put the window down.

So much for his theory that it was a guy who'd done this dick move. He banged on the glass again, steam billowing from his nose from the freezing temperature.

Finally she lowered her window about a millimeter. She must've been one of those women—the kind who think every guy is out to hurt you. Sheesh, he'd had enough of paranoid chicks like that. The last gal he'd dated came out and told him it was only a matter of time before he hurt her, either physically or emotionally, because that's what guys do. *What the fuck?* Alas, she was sort of prescient with that comment—he no doubt did hurt her emotionally when he immediately broke it off, not even waiting for their cocktails to arrive. Who wanted to be with a kook like that?

He put his face close to the crack in the window and spoke.

"Look, could you move your car? You've sort of parked me in." He pointed over her roof at the SUV, looming like the Siamese twin to her car, they were so close together.

He could see through the window that she was furrowing her brows.

"Yeah, I'll move it," she said, pausing. "But next time could you please be considerate of others and only take up one parking space?"

Carter stopped in his tracks. Suddenly he no longer felt chilled, but instead was consumed by the heat of unrepentant fury igniting in his body like a fireball on a comet bursting through the atmosphere.

"Excuse me?" he said, emphasizing the first word, his voice rising an octave. He knocked on the window as if he needed to get closer access to her to be sure she'd actually had the gonads to say that to him. Because surely she hadn't. His thoughts were like a metal ball in a pinball machine that pings from place to place in a rapidly random yet violent way each time it hits a bumper and bounces elsewhere within its limited confines.

She cracked her window a tiny bit more. "I said, please, next time use one space."

He thought his head might erupt like one of those volcanoes where the top of the thing blasts right off of it from pent-up activity within its core.

"Are you fucking kidding me?" he said, his pulse escalating as if he'd raised his heart rate to 170 on the treadmill again. "You're telling *me* how to fucking park?"

She frowned. "Judging by how you did this time, it appears you need the advice."

He waggled a finger at her vehicle. "Says you, who shoved your car so far up my SUV's ass it's gonna have to crap it out."

"You left me no choice. This was the third time this week some selfish member took up two spaces during peak time here. I'm sick and tired of inconsiderate—"

"Selfish?" He paused, fixing his gaze on her as the first barbs of sunlight illuminated this, this, this Judge Judy bitch sitting before him making determinations about which she knew absolutely nothing. "Listen up, pork chop." He pressed his finger right up on the window as he glared at her, ready to pierce her with his own arrow, and she wasn't gonna like it. "Clearly you've been packing on the pounds, dough girl. Maybe you should try spending more time in there"—he extended his arm toward the gym, his hand trembling—"and less time out here picking fights with complete strangers."

Suddenly the woman rolled her window down the rest of the way. This was perfect. He was gonna give her even more of a piece of his mind and tell her where she could shove her arrogant presumptions. But before he got even a half a syllable out of his mouth, she reached her arm out and chucked her cup of coffee all over his ski jacket and gym shorts. Then she put the car in drive and pulled out before he even had a chance to retaliate. Not that he would have. But still.

And he heard her exclaim as she drove out of sight, "I'd rather be fat on the outside than ugly on the inside like you!" Which caused his soul to shrivel a bit. He couldn't blame her for saying that. He'd no sooner uttered those hurtful words to her than he knew he was a complete and utter horse's ass who deserved to be wearing a cup of not-yet-tepid coffee.

Ironic that he'd been shivering from the cold a few minutes ago, and here he was inadvertently heated up by the cup of relatively hot joe now dripping from him. *Keyrist*. This was precisely why he didn't deal with women to begin with: they were all irrational, hot-headed, and mean-spirited.

He took a few deep breaths, trying to calm himself down, limped to his car on his lame ankle, unlocked the door to his SUV with the key fob, and gingerly climbed into the driver's seat. It wasn't till he stuck the key into the ignition that he noticed her note on the other side of his windshield, staring at him across the dashboard. He scanned her little nastygram:

CONGRATULATIONS! YOU'VE BECOME AN HONORARY MEMBER OF THE "PARK LIKE A JACKASS" CLUB. HERE'S HOPING SOMEDAY YOU REDEEM YOURSELF BY LEARNING HOW TO STAY IN THE LINES.
(PS: Your car reeks)

Damn woman got the last word on him twice. Well, that would be the last time he let some type A jerk like her get under his skin.

Chapter Three

CONSIDERATE of others? *Considerate of freaking others?* Was she joking? He was the one who stopped at every crosswalk during peak season when a bazillion annoying tourists disobeyed the traffic signals and jumped in front of cars to get across the beach road. God forbid they miss a minute of sunbathing. He was the one who once pulled over to help a turtle cross the road and get back to the water, so that it wasn't crushed by a vehicle. He was the one who once missed an important job interview because he helped rush his neighbor, who was in early labor and whose husband was out of town, to the hospital.

Inconsiderate, my ass.

Carter continued ruminating on that wretched woman—except crap, she was kind of cute, which he hated to admit. He was a sucker for an adorable blonde, with her hair pulled up in a high ponytail and those brown eyes. Give-you-shit eyes, they were. She seemed like one of those women who had an internal spark that ignites flames shooting sky-high when they're pissed. Which isn't necessarily the best of personality traits, but nevertheless it was sort of a turn-on. Those types of women were always a challenge, and damn if a woman who stirred the pot didn't stir his libido a bit too.

Granted it had been barely dawn when this all unfolded, but he could see her brown eyes smoldering and, well, as furious as he was, damn, he was intrigued. After all, it took some serious balls to toss her coffee on him. Some might say that was a bitch move, but in her defense, she was probably entitled to be a little aggressive.

If he was going to be honest with himself, his degree of assholeness was pretty much inexcusable. Here was this cute girl and he had to be a dick about it, had to go for the jugular. He knew—*he knew!*—how hurtful it was when someone criticized your weight. He remembered the pain his sister Madison had gone through in middle school when the mean girls would say things on Facebook about her being pudgy. Not that Maddie was that way anymore, but still. That stuff stuck with you.

Yet here he was being a damned mean girl like those bitches at his sister's middle school. What a fucking douche he was. As soon as he'd spoken the words, he'd wanted to stuff them back into his mealy mouth. But it was too late. The woman had pulled out with tires squealing, hollering out the window as she left, "I'd rather be fat on the outside than ugly on the inside like you!"

And she was right. He *was* ugly on the inside. And he was letting his lifestyle of burning the candle at far too many ends get to him—no sleep, lots of stress, and no sex was starting to turn him into a veritable ogre. The one thing that was keeping him sane was his daily workout, and now that one respite in his life was jeopardized. He was too embarrassed to return to the gym for fear he'd see her there again. Meanwhile he was starting work at a new restaurant tonight and was going to have to be "on" and cheerful, so he needed to get his collective shit together and stop being so dour.

He thought about that sexy little diamond stud in her nose and the only thing he could think about was how much he'd have loved to trace his tongue along it, maybe continuing down to the column of her neck. Yet more of an indication—if he was concocting sexy scenarios with the woman who'd angrily dumped her coffee on him this morning, he hadn't been laid in far too long. He needed to stick to focusing on work and get his mind out of the never-gonna-happen department.

He stopped to grab some coffee and a doughnut—because, well, doughnuts—when his sister called, speak of the devil.

"What's goin' on my sissy from another missy?"

She laughed. "Wait a minute. We have the same mother, you bonehead!"

He rested his phone between his head and his shoulder while he paid the cashier, then grabbed his doughnut and coffee cup as he walked out the door.

"Yeah but I'm the much better-looking child, so I figured I must come from entirely different stock."

"Oh, don't worry, you did. Livestock." She cackled into the phone, letting out a loud moo.

"Maddie Henderson for the win." He climbed back into his SUV, trying to juggle too many things at once, so naturally his doughnut fell to the ground. "Sonofabitch," he shouted into the phone. He didn't even have time to go back into the shop to replace it—the line was too long and he had too much to do. So he hopped out, picked up the doughnut from the dirty gutter, and wiped it on his coffee-stained jacket for good measure. This day got suckier by the minute.

"Hey, calm down. I was joking. You don't need to yell at me."

He knit his brows in a deep frown. "Sorry. Didn't mean that for you. I'm having one of those days. Anything that can go wrong has, and it's not even eight in the morning."

"That sounds a little drama-queenish."

"Trust me, it's not."

"Like what happened that could be so bad?"

"You do not want to know."

"Well, now you have to tell me. Spill it."

He heaved a sigh. "Fine. But if I do, then don't tell me I'm a big baby or that it's my own fault or anything like that."

"I totally reserve the right to do that."

"Maddie—"

"Oh, all right. Fine."

"First my battery died—"

"On Bertha?"

He laughed. For some reason, his sister had taken to calling his SUV by this name. He thought it had something to do with the vehicle being a substitute for a real woman, one with an ample rack, and a woman with huge tits would be called something like Bertha. He never knew where his sister came up with this nonsense.

"Yes. Bertha."

"Bertha been keeping you warm at night, Carter?"

"Shut up."

"I know. All I'm saying is you can actually make a

commitment to something more than an inanimate object with mag wheels and MacPherson strut suspension."

"What the ever-loving hell is MacPherson strut suspension?"

"Carter, Carter, Carter. You know me better than to ask me that sort of question."

It was true. She was the font of all knowledge and had been a champion trivia game player since she was about ten. He didn't ever dare challenge the extensive, but shallow, reams of useless facts at her fingertips. "To be honest, I don't know. I heard that term and thought it sounded good. So what else? Because a dead battery is not a deal-breaker for the day. It's a small inconvenience."

"Next I plowed down a skunk. Stench still lingering on the truck. Had to take two spaces at the gym—"

"Seriously? You're one of them? I hate people who do that."

"Do you think I did it to be an asshole?"

She remained silent.

"Fine, I know what you want to believe, but the answer is no. It was the last space and someone had parked over the line, so I had no choice."

"Okay but still, not the end of the world."

"But then some woman got all up my ass about my parking job and well, I said some inappropriate things, and it was kind of ugly and now I feel bad."

"What'd you say to her?"

"This is where you do not want to know. Trust me on this."

"Carter?" She dragged out his name to be like four syllables long, and her voice reminded him of when his mother used to bust him getting into trouble when he was a boy. Before she skipped out on all of them, that is.

Maddie would not let up until he confessed. She was relentless that way and would have been a great interrogator for a spy agency. She wouldn't have even needed to shove bamboo needles underneath prisoners' fingernails. She could hover disapprovingly, arms crossed, toe tapping in impatience, and get her answers. She'd make a great mom someday.

"Okay, okay. It was not my most shining of moments. I was tired. I was mad. Oh, I forgot to mention that I twisted my ankle on the treadmill and now I'm limping."

"Playing the world's smallest violin."

"And then some old gal dropped her dumbbell on my finger."

"What a dumbbell!"

His sister had the most idiotic sense of humor. And she probably got it from him.

"Already thought that one, so I beat you to it."

"So what did you say to the woman who was mad about your crap parking job?"

His voice lowered to a barely audible level and he speed-spoke his confession. "I might have suggested she should spend more time at the gym getting rid of her body fat than spending it fighting strangers in the parking lot."

Maddie gasped. "You jerk!" She started tsking him and he hated when she tsked him. "How could you be so cruel? I seriously would slap you if you were in front of me. That is your biggest asshole move in decades."

He didn't know he'd had enough dick moves to

quantify them as such.

"Look, Mads, I know, I know. I no sooner shouted it than I wanted to punch myself in the face for it. It was a lousy thing to say, and believe me, if I could, I'd take it back."

"Well then find the woman and take it back. And buy her a nice dinner to apologize."

He coughed out one of those "as if" sort of laughs. "Oh, right. I'll go out and search for a needle in a haystack." He took a swig of his coffee, but now, the mere idea of coffee was tainted with the events of this morning, so he rolled down his window and spat it out. Instead he took a bite of his dirty doughnut, only to realize it had sand grit all over it. Of course it did; he lived at the damned beach. "I know. Maybe I'll go hang out—during all my free time—at the gym until she comes back. And with any luck, she'll have some more coffee she can throw on me."

"What?" Maddie's voice went high and she stretched out another word into a couple of syllables.

"Oh, I forgot to tell you. She chucked her coffee all over me."

"Wow. I totally love this woman. Who is she? I've gotta meet her. She sounds so kick-ass."

"Um, whose side are you on?"

"Dude. You didn't just ask that. Because you don't want to know if you don't already. I love you dearly, but you are so at fault and I'm pretty mad that you did this. I'm gonna give you a couple of pity points because I know you've got a lot on your plate and you're probably tired, and best I can tell, you haven't hooked up with a female in an eternity." She paused. Carter hoped maybe she got disconnected and he could put this conversation to bed. "And I gotta say, if this is how you interact with women, well, it's no wonder."

He sighed. No such luck on her cell phone dropping her.

"Thanks tons for the unconditional support."

"Oh, you have that from me, but I'm going to withhold it for a while. See, you have to redeem yourself before I'm going to dole any of that your way."

"Doesn't that make it un-unconditional if you do that?"

"Uh, no. It means these are my rules. But I have a brilliant idea."

Carter shook his head. It was early enough that traffic wasn't congested on the beach road yet, which was one thing working in his favor. That said, off-season at the beach wasn't exactly overrun with rush hour traffic. "Great, princess. What's your Einstein plan?"

"Why don't you go to the gym and tell them what happened and say you want to apologize and maybe they could look at the tapes in the parking lot. I mean surely they have a security camera there, right?"

Ugh. The last fucking thing he needed to do right now was spread the word that he had been such a rat fink. The gym would probably kill his membership. Besides, seriously? Who is going to pore through hours of footage for that? He was gonna have to let this ride and hope like hell he never saw her again.

"Right. I'll get right on that. Meantime, any idea how to get coffee stains out of a down jacket?"

"You're not gonna do that, are you?"

"Track down the video footage of the crime? Hell

no." He was already late getting back to his place to start working on the books for a local woodworker. He needed to get caught up on that and steal a quick nap before he had to show up at the new restaurant for his first dinner service. Actual bedtime was not going to happen till about two in the morning.

"I'm gonna stick a pin in your voodoo doll, you know."

He rolled his eyes. His sister thought it would help people behave better if they thought they were getting some voodoo curse put on them. "Do me a favor and stick it in my left ankle, so maybe it'll undo the damage I did this morning. Sort of voodoo reverse psychology."

"In addition," she continued, "in order for me to forgive you, you are going to have to come to my place on three separate occasions with both dessert and chocolate martinis. Oh, and you have to agree to participate in the bachelor auction I've organized for the upcoming Community Services Organization fundraiser. We're raising money to fund a shelter for abused women and children."

Carter heaved a sigh. Was this what it was going to take to get his sister off his back? "Seriously? You know how much I hate stuff like that. It's humiliating. A bunch of drunk women treating you like man-meat, practically wanting to shove bills down your crotch."

"So maybe you'll find yourself a drunk woman with loose morals who will go home with you and then you can get some of that testosterone rage taken care of, so you don't insult sweet women at the gym next time."

"Seriously, Mads. You strike a mean bargain. As if my day hadn't already sucked, now this. I've gotta run.

Love you, Mads!" And before she had a chance to stick anything more in him, he pressed the red button and ended the call. You know the day sucks when even your sister hates you.

Chapter Four

JAMIE was an easygoing girl. She didn't usually let things get to her, so she tried to logically analyze why the jerk who'd co-opted the pair of parking spaces had made her so mad.

In reality, was she projecting her anger at herself for having allowed the stress of her parents' unpleasant divorce to weigh so heavily on her that she'd started to gain weight? It wasn't like her to be as tetchy as she'd been. But then, well, when he said that to her, was she going to sit there and let this stranger insult her? Hell no! She was glad she'd had that coffee to toss on him, or she'd likely have hauled back and punched the guy. Her guns were getting stronger each day at the gym, so it could've done some damage. She wished.

But then again, geez Louise! Dumping coffee on him seemed a bit, well, intense. Not to mention stupid. These days you never know what jackass is packing heat and would pull it out and shoot you. Not that this was what you normally encountered in her pokey little hometown of Verity Beach. The biggest drama around here would be a dead shark washing ashore.

The locals tended to be super chill, at least the ones she preferred. Most of the time, she hung with the types of people who naturally gravitated toward being kind and loving. As an artist, her tribe were fellow right-brain types, and she'd yet to meet an artist who would have even *noticed* she'd gained weight, let alone hurled it at her as an insult. Aside from hanging with those peeps, when not throwing clay as a potter, she was, for a good three-quarters of the year, beach bound and on a surfboard. And as far as she knew, there were no surfers who would be so hurtful. Those folks were happy in their own world and didn't care if her ass had gotten fat or sprouted a pair of horns, for that matter.

Though she had to be honest with herself: this state of disrepair was a new thing for her. She had always been lean and fit; you sorta had to be to surf. But in the past half year or so, as her parents dismantled their marriage while trying to take potshots at one another and buy their daughter's love with stupid materialism, it seemed like all Jamie could do was stuff her stress with an extra slice of pizza, a biscuit or two at breakfast, and maybe a carton of Ben and Jerry's Phish Food in between generous portions at mealtime.

Oh God. Phish Food. Manna from heaven. With that amazing vein of marshmallow twining alongside golden swirls of caramel, all swimming in an ocean of rich, chocolatey ice cream... Not to mention those fudgy fish, which were their own special mouth surprise each time you bit down on one. It all blended together to make a true slice of heaven on earth. Phish Food was the near-perfect dessert concoction.

And the thing is, it came in those dinky little containers, so it was super easy to have a spoonful and then another spoonful and then maybe another. And then your mother would call and complain about your father and that would be two more fat spoonfuls. Then your dad would call to ask if your mother was sleeping with the guy who owned the Surf Shack. As if a guy half her age would be caught in bed with her. Oooh, two more spoonfuls for the horrifying notion of her mother having sex with anyone, let alone Robbie MacIntyre, who was cute and charming and far, far too young for her mother. Ugh. Well, there you have it: the way her life had been going, it wasn't even hard to finish off a container of that shit without thinking twice.

Jamie hung her head sheepishly as she sat in her cute little beach bungalow alone, chewing on her lower lip and staring out into the stark winter sea mulling this awful turn of events. It didn't help that she couldn't get the ice cream off her mind and was desperate to dig into a pint of it even though it was breakfast time, and she had a hard and fast rule against ice cream for breakfast. Ish.

But she craved it so desperately. Because Phish Food was almost better than sex. Maybe actually better than sex. It was a toss-up. And since she had, of late, been wandering alone in what could be described as a veritable sexual desert—that is, in a super hostile environment with none available as far as the eyes could see—well, no wonder she was opting for dessert instead. Sooo ironic, considering she'd been double-dipping for a while there. Not with ice cream, but with men.

Right around the time her folks split up, she was happily dating two different guys, and the great thing was, neither one cared about the other! For that matter, she was even fooling around with both of them, and it was all on the up-and-up. It wasn't that she was easy-peasy or anything, but they were both super nice and gorgeous and, well, available. And didn't God invent condoms for this very reason? Besides, she was in desperate need of some sort of affection. After all, you can't be an unwilling foot soldier in your folks' conjugal war without needing an outlet of some sort. For her, that came in the form of Nick LeGrange and Toby Thompson.

She was friends with them from surfing—they were the type of guys who followed the seasons in order to continue with outdoor activities as much as possible. She'd been perfectly honest with them both that she was attracted to them and had zero interest in a relationship— witnessing the decimation of your parents' nuptials in a funeral pyre did that to you—but she enjoyed their company and friendship. And smoking bodies.

It was fine while it lasted, but after the season, they'd both moved on—Nick had gone to Aspen to be a ski instructor, and Toby was surfing in Indonesia or something exotic like that. So the men were gone, surf season had ended, her creativity seemed to have been sucked dry with her recent stress, and the only thing left to seek solace in seemed to be food. She was fully aware of it—she would catch a view of herself in the bathroom mirror and cringe at how chunky she looked all of a sudden. As if she was growing an extra her. But to have a complete stranger point out that she'd become a fat cow, well, she was still stunned by it. She could hardly blame herself for tossing coffee on him even though she was mortified she'd taken such action.

A tiny bit of her half wanted to apologize to the guy, but the other part wanted to smack him upside his head.

Which also didn't seem the civilized thing to do. She only hoped she would never see him again. Which of course was not a good thing because this would certainly deter her from attending the gym. She'd be peering around corners for fear of running into him again. Ugh. Too damn embarrassing. She hoped she'd get some exercise moving her hand from the ice cream pint to her mouth because that was the extent of the workout she was going to indulge in now. No doubt, the whole gym would laugh at her jiggly ass once they got wind of her encounter.

She was kind of scared at how ugly the guy had been toward her—he was positively feral with rage. Amazingly, he hadn't frothed at the mouth like a rabid dog. She hadn't experienced that much random yelling in her life except—except when her father and mother decided to split. Jesus, the screaming matches she was privy to. The words exchanged were downright unprintable.

That, in itself, was weird. For a long time, they seemed fine together. At least it had appeared that way from the outside. But then her father hit some stupidly annoying male midlife crisis and decided he was going to have sex with the new housekeeper. How cliché. You'd think he could have at least been creative about it. But no, instead, cue the old-dude-with-saggy-ass-finds-impoverished-young-hottie-to-bang-in-a-flattery-and-cash-transaction, and… that would be her dad. Whomp. Super icky, made all the worse because the girl—Ginger was her name, she was fairly certain—was Jamie's age. Double ugh. What was it with men and their dicks?

No wonder her mother was apoplectic when she

found out. Not only had she lost her husband, but she'd lost a good housekeeper to boot. That part made Jamie laugh. How typical of her mother—always bemoaning how hard it was to find good help. This time, the help was certainly no help.

Her father didn't have half a leg to stand on—making lame excuses for his errant behavior, rather than falling on his sword and apologizing till his dying day to her mom as he should have. Which was what launched the great saga of Lundquist vs. Lundquist, a seemingly endless legal war of ugliness that had scooped her up like one of those miles-wide fishing nets that aim to catch tuna but also entangle and destroy thousands of other fish in the process.

At first, Jamie was empathetic with her mother. How could she not be, what with her father's betrayal? But then her mother wouldn't buffer Jamie from their personal business, instead incessantly calling to bitch about how her father canceled her credit card, or how he'd be out at the country club till all hours while she had no life, or of course *that woman*. There was no end to the lamentations over the dreaded housekeeper. In the midst of it all, he forced her to close down the art gallery she'd run for fifteen years—meaning, Jamie's good friend Cameron's art got pulled, which made her feel bad since she'd had it displayed there in the first place.

Her mom had presumed that Jamie wanted to take on a participatory role in the divorce when frankly, it wasn't her monkey and it wasn't her circus. Or at least it shouldn't have been. But as the only child, it became her cross to bear. And it seemed the cross currently weighed an extra twenty pounds worth of Phish Food converted to blubber, spread out unattractively on her ass, hips, and thighs, dammit.

So after experiencing months of the shouting and hurling and ugliness at home, she suspected that jerky parking lot hog's yelling at her triggered some sort of PTSD response. It's like when the doctor taps on your knee with that little rubber thing: your leg goes flying and you kick him in the groin. You can't help it!

Well, with a little bit of luck, she'd never see the guy again. In the meantime, she made a mental note to be kind to strangers even if they might be complete pricks. You never know, and it's not worth risking being picked on for being a cow. It was too darned hurtful to take that chance again.

She looked at her watch and frowned. She needed to get to the restaurant or her dad would have her head. He'd recently brought her on to waitress at his new restaurant to teach her responsibility or some stupid nonsense like that—please, the man who fucked the housemaid teaching responsibility? But she figured it was a way to make some nice tips, chat it up with the locals who were coming in for a bite to eat. He'd alluded to "someday this will be yours" baloney, but she wasn't hearing it. Her father had turned on a dime with her mother, and if he could betray her, well, there was no telling whether he'd do so to her as well.

Chapter Five

CARTER was stoked. He'd been thrilled to land the job at Red Fish Blue Fish, as it was *the* place that all the locals went for the freshest seafood and had built a reputation in its short life as the best restaurant in town. Starting here in the off-season would give him time to get his sea legs. The restaurant turned about a 180 tables on a busy summer night and he needed the chance to get up to speed before he was expected to get to that level. He knew he could do it, but there would be a learning curve. This was his big chance to prove himself and his skills, and he felt lucky that the owner, Frank, was willing to give him a chance. If things went well, he could give up the side jobs and focus on what he now knew he was meant to do.

He pulled into the parking lot of the seaside establishment and was grateful that Frank wanted him to start tonight. It was a Monday, usually their slowest night. He'd been cooking long enough that he shouldn't be nervous, but this was his big break, and he didn't want to fuck it up. Easing in slowly would help him feel a bit more confident about things.

As he threw the truck into park, his phone rang. He looked at the screen and frowned—his father. Which no doubt meant he was about to hit Carter up for rent money or something. Carter was so damned sick of his father's irresponsibility. He wished he were able to compartmentalize it and let the guy sink or swim on his own. Curse him for having a soft heart and caring about the downtrodden.

He mulled whether to hit decline on the screen, but guilt got the better of him and he answered it.

"Hey, Dad." He swallowed against the sour taste that charged up his throat whenever these calls foisted themselves on him.

"Son."

There was silence on the line as Carter waited for him to go on.

His father cleared his throat.

"Dad?"

"Son, I hate to bother you but—"

Carter shook his head. *But.* He ought to start calling the guy "But" because that was the word most commonly uttered from his lips.

"Yeah, I think I've heard that a time or two."

"You see, my rent's due and I'm just scraping by."

"I thought you were doing better, Dad." Carter scrubbed his free hand over his face. He fucking hated these calls. "What happened to that construction work I found for you?"

His father hacked a few times, a phlegmy cough that told Carter he'd also been sick and not treated for whatever it was.

"That work's dried up."

Carter shook his head. "That's impossible. I was down the highway the other day and passed by that big construction site. There were plenty of workers out there, even in the cold of January."

"I was told they didn't need me."

Carter heaved a sigh. "So, you got fired."

"I like to think of it is as unhired."

"Jesus, Dad." Carter's voice lifted an octave. "I mean really. I do my damnedest to help you out of every mess you find yourself in and then you get yourself into another one."

"I'll make it right this time, I promise. But in the meantime, could you float me enough so I'm not out on the street?"

The whole thing pissed Carter off, and it was all he could do not to slam his fist on the steering wheel. His dad wouldn't be out on the street if he weren't such a slacker. What's worse is that all those years ago, once his mom had left, his father sort of gave up and left Carter and his sister to fend for themselves. So Carter had taken on the role of mother and father, in addition to big brother for his sister. And the older he got, the more he also had to be father to his father, which sucked massively.

He tried to tell himself he had to teach the man to fish, not only give him handouts. But then he felt worse. And shit, he found him jobs and still the guy couldn't sustain himself. He shook his head, squeezing his eyes shut as he pressed his temples with his thumb and pointer finger.

"I'm kind of in a hurry, so maybe cut to the chase and tell me exactly what you want."

"Five hundred is all I need."

This time, which was what burned his ass so much.

The next time would be looming right around the corner because his dad's affliction was being a thief who creeps inside in the dark of night, robbing you of your relationships, your dignity, your will to operate as a functioning human being. It didn't have to be that way. And why the hell did Carter think it was his responsibility to right his wrongs?

"Okay, I'll lend it to you, but I'm taking it straight to your landlord." He scratched his beard stubble with his hand. "Because you remember what happened last time?"

"It was all an accident, Carter. If that horse had won, I'd have doubled my cash."

"And if my aunt had balls, she'd be my uncle." He shook his head as he stared out the window at the beach in front of him. Sometimes his father made him want to go running far, far out into that ocean and not turn back to get away from his dad's crap. "I'll run the money by your landlord as soon as I can. And please, can you try to get your shit together for once?"

He didn't even say a formal goodbye but rather abruptly ended the call. Taking several deep breaths, he tried to eradicate his "dad stress" from his brain. He didn't want to drag that gunnysack of troubles into his happy place in the kitchen.

Any errant thoughts about his pain-in-the-ass father evaporated as soon as he slipped in the back door of the restaurant. A broad smile spread across his face as he once again beheld the beautiful space that was to be his new playground. A proper kitchen with room to move and stations to work without having another line chef practically up his ass was going to be amazing.

"Carter!" His new boss greeted him with a pat on the

back. "You're early! I wasn't expecting you for another half hour. Welcome."

"Thanks." No way was Carter going to be anything close to late—he wanted Frank to be certain that he could rely on Carter under any circumstances. "I tend to like to get in early so I can assess the situation and be ready for anything unexpected that might crop up."

"You won't find me complaining." Frank shook his head. "My last chef wasn't much of a clock-watcher, unfortunately, and sometimes would come breezing in here minutes before the dinner service was about to begin, expecting his kitchen to pick up his slack. Brilliant chef, shit employee."

"Been there, done that with other chefs, which is why that is something I'd never foist on my staff."

"Well, then good. I think we'll get along famously. I know you already met most of the staff when you were here last week, so I'll leave you to it."

That was fine by Carter. Once he unpacked his knives and got to work, he was in his comfort zone and nothing—and no one—would rattle him once he was in the zone.

Chapter Six

JAMIE drove a little too fast down the ocean road, racing to get to work before her dad flipped out on her. Still lost in thought over that jerk—her brain didn't seem to want to let it go—she wasn't focused enough on driving. Out of nowhere, a deer ran out into the road in front of her and she swerved to avoid it, but barely clipped the hind flank of the animal. Luckily the beach road speed limit was twenty-five, and even if she was speeding at thirty, it wasn't enough at that angle to have killed the thing. But she felt awful and pulled over immediately, hoping she could check to see if the deer was okay.

Ugh. How was she going to coax a frightened, wild deer into letting her check it out? What a preposterous notion that she could do that. But then she looked over on the passenger seat at the big bag of carrots that were taunting her—the ones she hadn't eaten because instead, she'd grabbed a bag of Doritos as a snack. Because who likes carrots? Um, definitely not Jamie. But maybe a scared deer?

She pulled the carrots from the bag and quietly approached the deer, which was standing on the edge of the road. Poor baby must've been terrified. Jamie made some soft clucking noises and extended her hand with the carrots in them as a peace offering.

The deer stared at her but didn't run off, which she hoped didn't mean it was wounded but rather trying to assess the situation. She inched closer to it, then held a carrot in the tips of her fingers, whispering encouraging words.

"Come on, sweet thing. That's it. You can do it." She spoke soothingly, her voice calm and quiet as she urged the carrot toward the animal.

"I'm so sorry. I didn't mean to hurt you. Are you all right?" She stepped closer, hopeful the deer wouldn't bolt.

"Here. I'm sharing my meal with you. Because it's healthful and nutritious, so I knew you'd want it." She didn't dare mention how happy she was to unload the food on an animal that might prefer it to Doritos.

The deer took a hesitant step toward her, then another. Jamie had the light on her phone turned on so she could shine it on the deer's flanks to see if there was damage. It didn't look like the impact even broke skin, which made her feel much better.

"Oh, what a good girl you are!" She wasn't up on her deer sexing but figured that since it didn't have a big rack on its head, it was a girl. Funny how in humans, a big rack meant it was a woman, but in deer, it meant a boy. Go figure.

The deer nibbled on the carrot in her fingers for a few more seconds then turned and leapt away into someone's backyard. She hoped it would get safely home to its parents tonight. She took a look at the time on her phone and her stomach dropped: her dad was sure to give her a tongue-lashing if she ran into him at work.

Although the one upside to his banging the maid was that he had no leg to stand on when it came to respectability and virtuosity. So, if he called her out for being late, she only had to remind him of Ginger and that pretty much shut him up. Good old-fashioned guilt was a marvelous currency in which to traffic every now and then.

She decided to enter through the front of the restaurant in hopes that her father would be in the back. She'd missed the staff supper, so he must've already realized she wasn't there. At least once customers started arriving, he'd have to bite his tongue rather than reprimand her out on the floor. She raced through the front entrance, said a quick hello to Olivia, who was on hostess shift tonight, and apologized to the rest of the waitstaff for her tardiness. When she explained about the deer, they were all understanding. It was still ten minutes until they would seat anyone, so she acquainted herself with the specials for the night as she tied on her apron.

"Did you meet the new chef?" Olivia said, rubbing her hands together greedily. "He's ho-ot." She drew out the word into two syllables.

Jamie lifted an eyebrow. "Right? That's good news, considering the last chef was old, cranky, and had a beer gut you could've served cocktails on."

"Well, I call dibs on the newbie, so keep your grubby paws off of him. Capiche?" She winked at Jamie.

"Oh, honey, you can have him. The last man I'd want to be with is a guy who works the hours that a chef works. I mean, I'm here now out of some sick sense of responsibility to my father or something, but no way would I want a career working past midnight each night and being stuck here on holidays and weekends. He is all yours."

"Yeah, well a chef can cook."

"This is true."

"So, imagine the amazing meals he'd make for you all the time. That would be my dream come true. Especially since I can't even boil water."

"Meh. Boiling water's so overrated. Though you've got a point. Imagine how sweet it would be to have a guy cooking fabulous dinners twenty-four seven. Except that he'd never be around twenty-four seven because he'd be at the damned restaurant all the time."

"Must you harsh my buzz so quickly? I was fantasizing about Carter and me and maybe a chocolate soufflé and, well…"

"So, you've gone straight to the food sex with him?"

"Hello, duh."

"Honestly I've forgotten all about sex and only focus now on the food. Maybe that's not such a good thing."

"Ya think?" Olivia tucked her long, straight black hair behind her ear. "Well, don't forget to go introduce yourself before things get crazy."

As much as Jamie's curiosity was piqued about this new guy, she so didn't want to encounter her father. Still, she'd have to man up and deal with it. What was he gonna do—fire her? Besides, it made more sense for her to make her appearance back there in front of everyone. Maybe he'd keep his mouth shut. For once.

She pulled her hair back into a ponytail as she made her way to the kitchen. She bumped it open with her hip—see, a little extra padding was beneficial for some things—and saw her father standing near the salamander broiler, head down in discussion with the man who must be the new hire.

"What up, James?" Jimmy, one of the line chefs, fist-bumped her.

"Dude. How was your day off?" The restaurant was closed on Sundays, so she loved to catch up on everyone's dish after the weekend had ended.

"Slow. Slept, drank a lot of beer. Watched a lot of football. You?"

"Meh. It was fine. Nothing too exciting."

Her father looked up, his face pinched with disdain.

"So thoughtful of you to deign us with your presence, Jamie."

She curled her lip. "What's new with Ginger, Pops?"

It's all she had to say. As an added bonus, she knew he hated when she called him that.

His brow furled. "Enough with the smart-ass comments. I want you to meet the new head chef." He reached for her elbow and pulled her over toward the man whose back was to her.

"Jamie, this is Carter Henderson, who's taken over for Ralph—or was it Raymond? The guy who always showed up late. Like you."

She licked the tip of her finger and tapped the air, making a sizzling sound. "Touché. You showed me." She reached her arm out to shake hands with the new guy, who was turning toward her. As soon as she took one look at his face, she gasped. "You!" Her voice was so loud everyone in the noisy kitchen turned toward them.

The man's face turned ashen. "Oh my God. You?"

"What the hell is he doing in my restaurant?" Jamie shrieked as she spun on her heel toward her father. "How dare you hire this, this, this nasty, nasty man without consulting me?"

Her father squinted. "Uh, your restaurant? Last time I checked I was paying the bills, not you."

"Yes, but you told me someday this would be mine."

"And someday it might be. But right now, it's mine. And I'll ask you to treat Carter with the respect he deserves." He glared at her. "Now apologize for that offensive comment."

Jamie stood there speechless, her pointer finger aimed at someone—her father, the mean parking lot guy, hell, she didn't even know who, but she was almost frozen in place and didn't push it into either man's chest as she might have otherwise.

"Apologize? To this troglodyte? Are you mad? If anyone is going to apologize, it's him. He's the rudest, most unbearably unpleasant man I've ever met."

"Jamie, stop acting like your mother, all overly dramatic and histrionic. I'm sure there's some sort of misunderstanding here that we can figure out."

"Oooh, no. Uh-uh. There is no mistake here. This man is a bottom-feeder. A cockroach. Vermin. And I will not work alongside him." She untied her apron and threw it at her father. "You choose. Him or me."

Then she turned and stormed out the back door, wishing in hindsight she'd had another coffee she could have tossed on that jerk for good measure.

Chapter Seven

WELL if that wasn't the maraschino cherry capping the shit sundae that was Carter's day. What were the fucking chances? Here he'd found his dream job and he'd insulted the owner's—his boss's—daughter. Of all the people on the planet, it had to be her. Un-freaking-believable. And even more so because now that he'd enjoyed a better glimpse of her, wow. How could he have hurled insults at her?

She was downright gorgeous. Streaky blond hair pulled back in a ponytail, brown eyes that drew you in and left you wanting to know more about her. And she was far from fat, for what it was worth. Not that being fat was wrong anyhow. Carter wasn't that sort of guy to judge body size. Well, usually, anyhow. He figured he could no longer lay claim to that distinction anymore. Jerk. Nevertheless, she had the type of shapely ass any self-respecting man would love to grab hold of. Preferably while burying himself deep inside her. Of course, that wasn't going to happen. Ever. Not with that one. First off, he'd been such a prick to her and second, he was in her father's employ. And third, evidently, shit, they were business colleagues and he never, ever mixed business with pleasure.

He was tempted to run into the parking lot to try to make amends, but his number one priority had to be his job, and any minute, customers were going to start entering the restaurant and placing their dinner orders. He couldn't let emotions take over when he had to use logic and get through this night and deal with her later. That is if he even had a job once this evening ended.

He had to address Frank before this got any further out of control.

"Look, Mr. Lundquist," he said, wringing his hands.

"Frank." His boss gave him a knowing nod.

Carter nodded. "Right. Frank." He heaved a deep sigh. "So, about that."

Frank raised his hand in crossing guard stop sign motion. "Don't worry about her. She's cranky, but she'll be fine. She's like her mother like that. I've got a restaurant to run. I don't want to deal with needless daughter drama. Ignore it and it'll go away."

Carter shook his head. "But sir, er, Frank, she's right to be upset with me. We had a bit of a misunderstanding this morning, and I lost my temper and said some things."

Frank slapped him on the back. "No worries, son. No time for this right now anyhow—time to get to work."

Carter knit his brow. To be honest, it was kind of dickish of the guy to not stand up for his daughter. What the hell? It made him even more guilty about how he'd insulted her earlier. He was going to need to do something to rectify this situation. Just as soon as he got through dinner service.

Jamie was cooling her heels in the parking lot when her father came out to check on her.

"Okay, Jamie. Enough with the drama. We've got customers inside who want to order food. I need you out on the floor."

It was times like this that she wished she could breathe fire, like some fairy-tale dragon. Maybe singe what remained of her father's thinning head of hair for good measure. Burn off his eyebrows. She was so frustrated with his lack of compassion for her these days. What had gotten into him? He used to be a nice guy. But now he'd stood up for this stranger he'd hired and told her to knock it off?

Jamie shook her head. "I'm not going back in there. Not until you fire him."

Her father blurted out a laugh. "Are you kidding? I just hired the man. I'm sure nothing he said or did is a fireable offense, and I'm in no position to be high and dry minus a head chef because my little Boo Boo's sensibilities were offended."

He slipped into baby talk when referring to her as his Boo Boo. She wanted to clobber him.

"How can you defend him? He called me pork chop. Told me I was fat and needed to focus on working out at the gym."

"Stop being so sensitive. I'm sure it was a misunderstanding and he didn't mean anything insulting by it. Sometimes guys say dumb things. Chalk it up to a mistake that will never happen again."

Frank was mimicking her talking by flapping his fingers together, which really set her off.

"Jesus, Dad. Maybe you need a bit of sensitivity training. How can you be so callous toward your only daughter? Or maybe you're trying to double-down on that jerk's snide remarks." She pointed toward the restaurant. "Why don't you rename the restaurant the Beached Whale after me. You can put my picture on the sign for good measure."

Her dad rolled his eyes. "Okay, sorry your feelings were hurt. But you are my employee, and I need you in there working even if it means you have to lick your psychological wounds while you do it."

Jamie crossed her arms, determined to dig in. "Nope." She shook her head with a pronounced swish of her ponytail. "Not gonna do it. Not until you fire him."

His eyes bugged wide open. "I've got news for you, Suzy Sunshine. You are going to march in there and get to work or else I'm going to cut off your mortgage payments and you'll find yourself out on the streets in the cold, bleak winter."

Well, crap. Nothing like hitting her in the jugular. Jamie had enjoyed a good relationship with her parents before their whole marriage implosion. Until then, she'd remained living at home—the house was huge, so she could enjoy her own privacy, and it was right on the beach, with a gorgeous swimming pool, so what wasn't to like about the situation? But when they split, they sold the house, and her father essentially paid her off by buying her a cute beachside cottage which, by the way, she adored. Sure, she knew she was milking him emotionally when she got him to buy her place, but he owed her that much for having done what he did. Didn't he?

She clenched her teeth and pursed her lips. Her hands were fisted into tight balls and she wanted to jump up and down and scream and maybe even throw herself on the ground and pitch a temper tantrum like a two-year-old, but that didn't work so well once you were a grown-up. Even if you had been successfully manipulating your cheating father to exact revenge for having destroyed your family. Besides, the gravel parking lot was no place to hurl yourself onto the ground in a pique of rage. She squinted at Frank in her best stink eye glare and snarled.

"Fine. I'll go back in there, but don't expect me to be civil to that man. I won't even look him in the eye. And I'm putting you on notice that I'm doing this under deep, deep protest, and it's going to be a good, long while until I forgive you for not siding with me on this one. Frankly, I think you're being a lousy father. But if you're content to be that, then so be it."

She wiped her hands together as if she were dusting him out of her life, tugged on her bra, which had ridden up and was digging into the underside of her boobs, straightened out her black skirt, the waistband of which had also jimmied up her burgeoning belly, and turned her back on her father.

"And wait till Mom hears about this one."

Chapter Eight

ALL in all, Carter's first night went relatively smoothly. Well, aside from the situation with the gym girl. What was her name? Jamie? Setting aside that issue, he'd done okay. The kitchen got in the weeds for a short while between seven and eight o'clock, but it was nothing he hadn't handled before, and everything worked out fine. No one sent back any meals, things went smoothly with his staff, and his sous chef, a guy named Mack, was excellent, so he felt good about things.

When Jamie had returned to the kitchen shortly after she'd stormed out in a huff, she pulled Carter aside for a fleeting moment. He'd hoped it was to bury the hatchet, but it was more like she whacked him over the head with it instead.

"Look," she said, her slitted eyes making it abundantly clear she wasn't there on a peace mission. Poking him in the chest with her forefinger drove the point home further. "I'm not happy about your being here. But I have no control over this situation, so I'm stuck dealing with it, like it or not. But understand: there is to be not one word spoken to me. Not a word. And don't even look at me. Do you hear me?"

Oh, he heard her all right. And unfortunately, since

she was so close to him, he could also see the golden flecks of caramel in her eyes that seemed to spark alongside her flaring temper. And as he stared at her face, he couldn't help but notice her full, pink lips and wonder what it would be like to place his own over them before running his tongue along them as he sought to gain entry to her mouth.

Jesus, he needed to get laid. If he wasn't careful, before he knew it, he was going to be fantasizing about the old lady at table eight who had insisted on regaling him with details of her angina when he went to check on their meals. Not that he could compare an octogenarian to this Jamie girl. She was spunky as hell, and damn if he didn't find that extremely attractive. It was probably a good thing she hated his guts because otherwise, he'd have a hell of a time sticking to his rule of no relations with work colleagues.

He wanted the chance to apologize to her formally, so before she slipped out unnoticed after closing, he approached her.

"Would it be possible to have a minute with you? Please?" He placed his hands in prayer position to emphasize his wishes. He was fully prepared to grovel his ass off if he had to, though he was afraid he was going to have to grovel to get a word with her, let alone get her to forgive him. What an idiot he'd been.

She glared at him. "I'm pretty sure I told you earlier not one word to me."

He held up his hands in surrender. "I know. I know. But please, if we're going to be working together can't you please give me a chance to explain myself a little bit? I promise I won't bite." He grinned, and she frowned.

"More importantly, I promise I won't say anything ugly."

She rolled her eyes. "Fine. I'll give you one minute. And then after that, no words to me ever again. Got it?"

Carter was grateful she didn't whip out her phone and set the timer for precisely one minute.

He looked around at the staff finishing cleanup in the kitchen. Not the place for this conversation. He reached for her elbow to guide her elsewhere, but she flinched at his touch. It made him feel all the more wretched. He'd never had a woman flinch at his presence before. It was punishment enough.

"Can we take this discussion to the office, please?"

She turned and walked to the office, stiff as a cadaver. Her body language was speaking volumes to him and everyone around them.

Once they were both in the office, he closed the door behind them. He dragged his fingers through his hair. Ugh, this was going to be an unpleasant minute of his life.

"Look," he said, heaving a deep sigh. "You've got every reason in the world to hate me. To want to smack me over the head with a frying pan—"

She nodded vigorously. "Brilliant idea. Remind me to grab one when we leave here."

While her words weren't too friendly, he took slight comfort that she responded at all. He offered a tepid smile.

"Be my guest." He scrubbed his face with his hands. "As I was saying, I completely understand your hating me and you're thoroughly justified in so doing. I was such an asshole and I'm really, really sorry. And I'm not only apologizing because your father is my boss. The moment I uttered those words, I wanted to smack myself for having said them. It was unacceptable. And they weren't even true. It was completely dickish of me. I get that. And if it would make you feel better to hit me with a frying pan, then so be it. Though you don't strike me as the violent type."

She pursed her lips. "What type do I strike you as?"

Oooh, this was a damned if you do, damned if you don't question. He bit his lip and lifted his eyebrows as he pondered this.

"Is 'no comment' a fair answer?"

She crossed her arms over her chest. "It's a cowardly one."

This woman was going to be the death of him. Cowardly? What the hell?

"Okay, fine. So if I had to pull one word out of thin air, I'd say judgmental."

She knit her brows. Clearly the wrong answer.

"Judgmental? Are you serious?"

"Look, you made me say something. I didn't know what to say. I only said that because you made presumptions about how I parked my truck that were based on nothing but pure judgment."

"Uh, yeah. Because you were smack dab in the middle of two spaces. It was so obvious you didn't want your car to get dinged by someone else's car door."

He held up a finger. "Or perhaps the car next to me had straddled spaces, so I had no choice but to follow suit. Did that ever cross your mind? Or were you too busy judging me?"

She toed the ground with the tip of her shoe, fixing her gaze downward.

"Ummm…"

"Ummm, yeah."

"Well, how was I supposed to know?" She looked up at him, her cheeks red with embarrassment. "Besides, that doesn't alter how you responded to me."

He held his hands up again. "Like I said, I'm sorry. I'm not that guy, the one who would be nasty to a complete stranger—or even someone I know, for that matter. I'd had such a crap morning and then you got all up in my face, and I lashed out at you." He rubbed his jawline with his hand. "And the thing is, well, look at you. You're a beautiful woman. Clearly you know what I said wasn't even true. It was a jerky guy striking out with an easy attack. Even though honestly, I'm not a jerky guy. And I feel like complete shit. And I never wanted to hurt your feelings. And my sister's super pissed at me if that helps."

"You told your sister what you said?" Jamie lifted an eyebrow.

He shrugged. "I had to. She makes me tell her everything. And she read me the riot act. I'm not even certain she's speaking with me at this point. Does that help?"

Jamie shook her head. "I don't know. This whole thing is kind of stupid. I mean, don't get me wrong, I totally hated you for that. It was plain mean. And yeah I have gotten kinda fat, but fuck you for pointing that out to me—"

He reached out for her hand, a pleading look in his eyes. "Seriously, don't take what I said as anything but the rantings of a man in instantaneous temper tantrum mode." He put the tip of his pointer finger beneath her chin and lifted her face toward his. "You're a beautiful woman. There is nothing about you or your body that you should be ashamed about. I'm the one who needs to be ashamed for how I reacted this morning. And believe me, I'm deeply remorseful." He gently ribbed her with his elbow. "Besides, I can assure you most men like women with a little extra junk in the trunk. Not that you have that, mind you." He quickly erased the comment with his hands in the air.

Jamie knit her brow and remained silent while Carter squirmed. At last, he couldn't wait any longer.

"So can we call a truce? Maybe start again. I think you'll find I'm not a complete asshole once you get to know me."

She huffed out a blast of air and shook her head. "Fine. I mean normally, I'm not one to hold a grudge, but wow, that was way beyond the pale. But I'll give you the benefit of the doubt and we can start from scratch. You're going to be working overtime to make up for this, though."

She scrunched her nose at him and tentatively extended her hand, which Carter gladly shook.

"I'm totally up to the challenge."

Now if he could eradicate from his mind that she was one of the most gorgeous women he'd had the pleasure of meeting in a long, long time... Because there was no way he'd ever entertain the idea of anything other than a cordial friendship with Jamie Lundquist. Of that, he could be sure.

Chapter Nine

CARTER knocked on the weathered door of his father's landlord's office.

A lanky man with thinning hair and kind, blue eyes opened the door.

"Carter." He reached out to shake his hand.

"Lou," Carter said. "Nice to see you."

"Likewise. You here about Edgar?"

Carter frowned. As if he wasn't always hearing the latest woes about the man. "Unfortunately."

Lou patted him on the back. "Man, I'm sorry about things."

Carter sighed. "I'm sorry. I hate that he keeps putting you in this position."

Lou knit his brow. "Huh?"

Carter pulled out his checkbook and pen, preparing to write a check. "Late with the rent again."

Lou held up his hands. "I didn't mean that," he said. "I was talking about his diagnosis."

Carter squinted at him. "What do you mean, diagnosis?"

"You mean he hasn't said anything to you?"

"About?"

"Carter, your father has lung cancer."

Carter's eyes grew wide with shock. "What are you talking about?"

"I'm sorry to be the one to tell you. But to be honest, you need to know anyhow. Yeah, it's been a week or so since I found out."

"How'd he learn this?"

"Some of these older folks who live here, well, we all know they're struggling financially. There's no safety net for many of them. We've got a few volunteers from the free clinic who check in on them and if they have reason to do further tests they'll take them into the hospital to learn more. It was a real cute woman doctor who was treating him and she was concerned at the sound of his lungs, took him in for X-rays and scans."

"What the fuck?" Carter pounded his fist on the wall. "He doesn't even tell me?"

"Sorry, man. I assumed he'd told you about it. But I'm glad you know now."

Carter was torn between being furious and upset. Edgar was his dad, after all. But he also was a constant emotional drain and had been for the better part of his life. He forever wrestled with feelings of guilt and obligation and worry and responsibility, and it all got tangled in a spiderweb of stress and ill will for him.

He scribbled out the information on the check, tore it out of the checkbook, and handed it to Lou. "I'm grateful to you for clueing me in. And sorry about Dad with the rent. Please keep me posted on things, so he's not floundering here, okay?" He wrote his number on a nearby notepad and handed it to him.

Next Carter returned to the car then carefully carried a large bowl of homemade chicken soup as he made his way down the dark hallway, along the dingy concrete floor to his dad's place. He hated to wake him if he was asleep, so he turned the handle in case it wasn't locked. Annnd, of course, it wasn't. Not that he'd have anything to steal were someone to break in, but still.

He peered inside and everything was dark even though it was midmorning. The room only had a few small windows and the shades were all drawn.

The sound of his father coughing in the bedroom let him know he was awake. Carter decided to go on in.

"Dad?" He poked his head through the bedroom door.

Although it was well after ten, his father was in bed. "Carter. Son. Good to see you."

"Hey. You too. Uh, you gonna tell me what's up with your health anytime soon?"

Edgar waved his hand as if swatting a fly. "Oh, it's no big deal. Didn't want to trouble you."

"Dad. Telling me you've got lung cancer is not troubling me. How long have you known and what has the doctor said?"

"Not long. Waiting to figure out a treatment."

"What's the prognosis?"

His father shook his head. "Who the hell knows? You know how these things go."

Carter pulled up a chair and sat down next to him. "No, actually, I don't. It's different for every person. And you want to get the best care you can because it can make a difference."

Edgar shrugged. "I've got what Medicare will give me. After that, it's a wing and a prayer."

"I'd like to talk to your doctor so we can figure out a

plan."

"Carter, this is my problem to worry about, not yours. Let me take care of dealing with it."

So now he finally becomes accountable for himself. Great damned timing.

"Nice idea, and I appreciate the sentiment, but when you're sick, you need family to help out. I'm going to call Maddie and we'll put our heads together and figure things out, okay?"

"Son, I know you're busy and I don't want to trouble you with my worries."

Carter wasn't one to get overly affectionate with his father. It was that way when you had to be your parent's parent for so long. But he did have sentimental feelings for him. He reached out and wrapped his hands around his father's. "With all of us working on this it will be much better than you trying to go it alone. We're a family. A highly dysfunctional one, maybe, but family nonetheless. Which reminds me, I brought you some chicken soup. You sounded bad on the phone, so I figured it might help. Not sure how much curative powers it has for what you've got, but I'll go put some in a bowl and bring it in here."

He helped his father sit up in bed and opened the shades to let light into the place.

He went to the small galley kitchen and found a pan, pouring some soup in to quickly reheat it. Rifling through the sparse contents of the cabinets, he found a large mug, which he figured would be easier than a bowl for eating. When the soup had heated sufficiently, he poured it into the mug, and grabbing a spoon, brought it to his father.

"See if this doesn't help at least a little bit. I'm going

to have to run because I've got to get to work, but call Maddie or me if you need anything. In the meantime, we'll get this medical information figured out. I put the rest of the soup in the fridge, so you've got more for later. Don't forget to eat it, you hear me?"

His father nodded and thanked him for his help.

Carter gathered up as much of his dad's medical paperwork as he could find and left. He gave his sister a call once back in the car.

"Hope you're making a fabulous dessert for Sunday night," she said as she answered the phone. "I'm going to dig up a really cute girl to come along just for you. You need to date again."

"I gave up girls for Lent," Carter said, laughing.

"It's not Lent for another month."

"I think it was last Lent, and I never started up again."

"I think that's called a dry spell, not self-sacrifice."

"Tomato, tomahto."

"Yeah, well. I'm expecting you to outdo yourself with your choice of desserts."

"My aim is true, Mads. But listen, we've got some trouble here. It's Dad. He's sick. I had to find it out from his landlord. But he's been diagnosed with lung cancer."

Maggie gasped into the phone. "Impossible. Despite his always leaning on you for everything, I always pictured him hanging on well into his nineties at least. What's the prognosis?"

"I haven't a clue. I grabbed a pile of papers from the hospital I found on the kitchen table when I was at Dad's place and was hoping you might take it all and start trying to figure things out. I'm swamped between all of my jobs."

"Dude, of course I'll do that for you. It's the least I can do."

"I'll swing by later this afternoon and drop it off. If you're not there, I'll slide it under your door. It'll be in a big manila envelope."

"I've got it under control. You go do your thing and let me spearhead this."

"You're the best, Mads."

"Right back atcha."

"So you're no longer ticked at me?"

"I'm able to compartmentalize. I'm like a guy in that way. Make me a good dessert, and don't forget the chocolate martinis, and then we'll talk contrition."

"Wouldn't forget for the world."

Chapter Ten

FOR the next several mornings at the gym, Jamie still tried to avoid being anywhere near the black SUV and inside the gym area. Better that she hide downstairs in the room with the spin bikes rather than working out on the floor with all the other equipment in plain view. She preferred to keep, damn, what was his name again? Carter? Yeah, she preferred to keep Carter at a distance. She couldn't *not* accept his apology, and he seemed truly sincere, but still, it was an awkward situation. Made all the more unfortunate with her father's complete void of give-a-care. What had gotten into him? It was beyond frustrating. Until recently, he'd been such a sweet, thoughtful, even doting father. Now it was all about him, and that didn't sit well with her.

It didn't help matters that upon further observation, she realized that Carter guy was kinda hawt. He had sandy-blond hair and those green eyes that were almost translucent—kind of like you couldn't hide your true nature behind those eyes. Best she could tell by his chef's garb, he looked fit, too, darn it. Well, there would be no gawking at Carter whatever his name was. Dude was 100 percent off limits forever.

On her way to a meeting about an upcoming

fundraiser she was helping with, her phone rang. A quick glance at the screen said it was Leslie calling.

"Hey, Mom," Jamie said as she put the phone to her ear.

"Jamie, dear," she said. "What's new with you?"

"Well, since we last talked, I had some jerk guy insult me at the gym for being fat, and I pouted and stress ate over it, then was late to work and Dad snapped at me, and who ends up being the new chef? The jerky guy."

"It figures your father would hire someone like that. I'm surprised he didn't hire the maid to cook for him. Though he probably doesn't have to pay for her to cook for free at home."

"I'm sure she's paying a steep price."

"Please, don't remind me that he's having sex with that thing. Such a shame because she did clean so thoroughly."

"She cleaned your clock is what she did."

"Yeah, that too. But I've decided I'm going to stop dwelling on that. If he wants to be with someone half his age, well, then so be it. And if she wants to be with some man old enough to be her father, well, clearly she needs therapy. Not my problem."

"Mother! How very mature of you." Jamie reached over to take a swig of water as she pulled up to a traffic light.

"Well, my friend Marcia has been taking me to meditation classes, and she's got me focusing on being mindful, and honestly it's hard work doing that. Because you know deep down I still kind of want to beat him senseless for what he did, but ultimately that doesn't do me any good, does it? I'd have much greater satisfaction if I grow as a human being as a result of this setback, rather than stoop to his level."

"Well, I'm very proud of you for this change of attitude. It will help me too, so I'm even more thrilled about it. Cause believe me, it's not been easy sitting on the sidelines of this war."

"Ha-ha, very funny. Now what's this about the chef insulting you?"

"It's a long story. But we've kind of ironed it out. I mean it's not like I'm going to date the guy ever, but I have to be pleasant around him or else Dad won't pay my mortgage."

Her mother laughed. "I guess we all have our price, don't we? But good for you not letting him get the better of you, darling."

"Look, Ma, gotta run. I'm arriving at my meeting now. Good luck taking the high road with Dad. I'm rooting for you."

Jamie was a few minutes late, so she settled into a folding chair at the back of the room, sitting next to a woman with the most beautiful greenish eyes and long, curly dark hair.

"Hi, I'm Maddie," the woman said to her in a whisper, offering her hand. "They've finished talking about some old business and now they're getting to the bit about the fundraiser."

Jamie nodded. "Thanks for the update. I think this is going to be a blast to put on."

"Right?"

They sat back and listened as the chair of the event discussed details and assigned people in attendance to various committees as they volunteered.

"I'd love to do recruitment," Maddie said. "Maybe we get first dibs on some of these guys that way."

"I like the way you think. Been through a bit of a dry spell, so maybe this is just the ticket to finding someone who'll oil the old joints."

Maddie laughed. "I'm sure there are loads of men who would be happy to oil your joints."

Jamie shook her head. "You'd be surprised. It seems they've all skipped town and I'm left to my own defenses. Which means I've forgotten what it's like."

"The good news is it's like riding a bike. Before you know it, you'll be right back on one and it will be second nature."

Jamie smiled. "I'm not sure if we're talking about guys or sex but either way, from your lips to God's ears."

Maddie nodded. "Both. I've been on the abstinence superhighway for far too long myself, so preach it, honey. Sadly the only men I've been with in forever are Ben and Jerry."

"What a coincidence. They're two of my closest friends as well. Who better to keep a lonely girl company on cold winter nights? Hey, you want to volunteer to work on the recruitment committee together? I get the feeling we'd have a great time doing this." Jamie held her thumbs up. "Plus it looks like no one is jumping to work on that one—all the old gals are steering clear of it. Which makes sense because we'd likely end up with their bachelor nephews who are in their sixties and like to do crossword puzzles for fun."

"Can't guarantee I won't end up finding someone equally unappealing, but I'll do my best to find a few good men who are auction worthy." Maddie's eyes lit up. "In fact... I've got the perfect candidate."

"Awesome—after we volunteer, why don't we leave here and grab coffee or something so we can brainstorm a bit."

"Change coffee to drinks and you're on," Maddie said, nodding vigorously. "Follow me to my place and we can get our recruitment on. Starting with my brother. He owes me, big-time."

Chapter Eleven

JAMIE followed Maddie back to her beach house, located on the sound side of the narrow peninsula that was buffered by ocean on one side, inlet on the other. Jamie preferred to live on the ocean side, but the sound was a little quieter, which had its advantages.

The neighborhood was a mix of weathered wood-sided houses and two-story condos surrounded by marsh and the sound, which extended for a good distance on the horizon. She remembered doing day camp out on the sound when she was little, learning how to sail the tiny Sunfish sailboats. It was a perfect place to do it because the water was generally calm, super shallow, and pleasantly warm, so even if you went overboard, it wasn't scary water at all.

She followed her new friend up a flight of steps to the second-story condo and Maddie stuck her key in the door to unlock it.

"Cute place you got here," Jamie said as the door opened and she scanned the cream-colored living room. It was quite minimally appointed but for a long cream sofa accented with bursts of color from a few paintings on the wall. "Oh my God! I totally recognize those paintings."

"You do?"

Jamie nodded. "They're from my mom's shop. My best friend painted them."

"She did?"

"Not a she. He. Cameron Sanders."

"That's so cool. And your mom owns the gallery?"

Jamie shrugged. "Well, she did. But it was a victim of collateral damage from the divorce, unfortunately."

"Such a bummer. I went there several times. Really liked the place. And your mom seemed so sweet."

"Yeah, well, she has her moments."

They walked to the kitchen where Maddie pulled a bottle from a rack in the pantry. "Red good for you?" Maddie opened the bottle and poured two glasses.

"As long as it's wine, I'm totally fine." Jamie reached for the glass as soon as Maddie handed it to her.

"Here's to a new friendship," Maddie said as they tipped glasses.

"And to our best boys, Ben and Jerry." Jamie broke out into a laugh.

"Indeed." Maddie walked them over to the bar overlooking the kitchen and grabbed both their coats, draping them across the dining room table nearby. "I want you to come back Sunday for drinks. My brother—the one I've wrangled into doing the auction—owes me, big-time, so he's going to bring dessert and make chocolate martinis. I think you'll like him. But if you do and you two hit it off, you have to promise to lend him to the auction anyhow—no proprietary claims of ownership if you start dating. Deal?"

Jamie laughed. "Trust me, the chances of anyone dating me right now are slim anyhow."

Maddie wrinkled her brow. "Why would you say that? I think you're awesome and so gorgeous too."

She shrugged. "Yeah, well, I've kind of porked out over the past six months and I can barely look at myself in the mirror, so hardly blame a guy for not wanting to."

Maddie twirled her pointer finger in a circle to the side of her head. "You, my dear, are loco. A guy would be lucky to have you as his girlfriend. You need to stop beating yourself up and appreciate your gifts!"

Jamie frowned. "I know. You're right. I've had a tough time of it over the past year. My folks split up and it pretty much undermined my sense of self in a way. The divorce has been unpleasant, and they've manipulated me at every turn to side with them. So, I decided to befriend food instead—much more reliable, won't betray you."

"I hear ya. Sadly my standing date with Ben and Jerry seems to be every night about eleven o'clock."

They both laughed. "You'd better watch out or I'll fight you for both of them."

"Maybe we need to recruit them for the auction. The girls would go wild."

"I wish. But shy of that, I suspect your brother will be a good start. I'm looking forward to meeting him." She waved her hand around the condo. "Your place is so soothing. So brave of you doing such a completely stainable color palette!"

"Yeah, well, I like to live life on the edge. I figure now's as good a time as any: no pets, no kids, the perfect time to not fear the complete ruination of my carpet and furniture."

"And particularly brave to plan for chocolate martinis."

"You'll have to promise not to throw them against the walls or anything." Maddie leaned her head against Jamie's as they giggled.

"Can't imagine anything that would even make me want to do such a thing."

"Yeah, well, you haven't met my brother."

Jamie lifted an eyebrow. "Problem child?"

"To the contrary. He's the golden child if anything. Honestly, he raised me. I owe him plenty. Though right now I'm sort of mad at him."

"What for?"

Maddie reached over the counter and pulled out a small, dark blue, knitted doll with button eyes and pins sticking out of it. She held it up. "He was being a jerk."

Jamie grabbed the thing. "So you have a voodoo doll and you stick pins in it to get even with him?"

Maddie nodded. "Yep. It's a little passive-aggressive. But more so, it's an inside joke."

Jamie knit her brows. "Does it actually hurt him when you do something?"

Maddie waved her hand. "Nah. It's simply for fun. I make my point with it. Point—get it?"

"Hilarious. Sooo… can I stick a pin in? Seems like it would be fun to do, under the circumstances, what with my man problems and all. Plus there's a guy I'm pissed at, so this can serve as my surrogate. I can take it all out on him."

Maddie handed her a pin. "Go for it."

Jamie grabbed the pearly head of the pin and jammed it into the crotch of the doll. "Going for the jugular," she said with a chuckle.

"You truly are exacting revenge on the male

gender."

Jamie shrugged. "Yeah, well, every now and then one of them deserves it. Though perhaps I'll have to apologize to your brother when I meet him for making him the scapegoat for the rest of them."

"Probably better to keep this between you and me. Bad enough he knows I do this to him, but if he knew I shared the love, well…"

"Mum's the word. And I'm sure I'll feel downright wretched once I meet him so would never want to admit it."

They tipped their glasses together again, laughing.

Chapter Twelve

CARTER was beat. It had been a long week, between getting to know the ropes at the new restaurant by night, continuing work on several side accounting projects by day, and starting to plan a new menu for Red Fish Blue Fish in between everything else. He'd decided to stay with the current menu until he got settled in, figured out how well the kitchen crew worked together, and what types of foods the customers seemed to prefer before making any dramatic changes. Sure, he wanted to put his imprint on the place, but as a diner himself, he always hated when new chefs made abrupt changes, and there would be time for that.

Frank had announced he was going to host a reception to formally welcome Carter as the new head chef of Red Fish Blue Fish, which didn't thrill Carter to tears. He hated being the center of attention. He'd much rather take care of business in the kitchen and let people enjoy his efforts while they break bread with their own family and friends without fawning over him. But it wasn't his to decide and it came with the territory, so he'd go along with the plan and try to blend in as much as possible.

For now, though, he was going to enjoy his day off

by cooking dessert for his sister as promised. He'd debated whether to make something super fancy or go for simple and settled on the latter. In truth, it gave him a chance to watch football for a couple of hours. Besides the prep involved, his initial plan of chocolate soufflés would've been too much alongside chocolate martinis. Instead he settled on a dessert he'd enjoyed years ago while backpacking through the English countryside called an "Eton mess."

His meringues had cooled off, and he'd found the best local cream to whip for the dessert; sadly there was no way to replicate the amazing cream you can find in places like Devon, England. As he whipped the cream, he added enough sugar to tickle the taste buds. He'd hulled his strawberries, pressing some to release the juices as they waited to be blended with the other ingredients.

Deciding not to serve it in individual glasses, he instead assembled it all in a large trifle bowl. He broke up the meringue into bite-sized bits and slowly layered the trifle dish with the whipped cream, meringue bits, and the macerated berries. He always loved this dessert because it looked such a mess but tasted divine. He continued layering until he reached the top of the trifle dish and surveyed his masterpiece. It looked as if someone had dropped the dessert on the ground, then scooped it back up into the bowl, hoping no one would notice. Perfect. It was far too much dessert for the two of them to eat, but it would be fun digging right into the bowl with spoons like they always did with this one. Besides, his sister had threatened to invite a friend to try to lure Carter in, so he wanted to be sure there was enough. Not that he was planning to succumb to his sister's manipulations, but still.

Maddie greeted her brother at the door with her hair pulled up in a towel.

"Thanks for going the extra mile to look good for your brother." The corner of Carter's mouth lifted into a wry grin.

"Anything for you, bruthuh," Maddie said as she freed his hands from the burden of the dessert. "This looks insanely delicious. Can I cut to the chase and dig in?"

He wagged his finger. "Not yet. We've got chocolate martinis to make first, lest we forget."

"I could never forget—they're my favorite."

Carter used his hip to open the door the rest of the way as he carried in the bags with the rest of his goodies inside them.

He lined up his essential ingredients on the kitchen counter: vanilla vodka, crème de cacao, Godiva chocolate liqueur, half-and-half, chocolate syrup, a chunk of chocolate, and his trusty Microplane zester to shave chocolate atop the drinks. He even remembered fresh mint leaves for a garnish. He rummaged around his sister's cabinets until he found the martini glasses and pulled two down.

"Ah, could you grab one more, please? I made a new friend I've invited over tonight."

Carter lifted his brow. "Huh. What's his name?"

She smirked. "Why do you presume it's a man? In fact, it's a woman. She's super fun and we're working on a project together. I thought you might enjoy meeting her."

Carter rolled his eyes. "Awww, Mads. I hate it when

you try to set me up. Last time you did that, I almost got arrested."

"I had no idea she was so young. She lied to me."

"Yeah, well, imagine how embarrassing it was for me when she got carded after I ordered us both drinks and she was rejected for being underage."

His sister shrugged. "It's not like she was seventeen or anything."

"She'd barely turned eighteen. A full eight years younger than me and was fresh out of high school. She was practically jailbait."

Maddie waved her hands. "Pish posh. Jailbait. What a bunch of malarkey."

"Says you who wouldn't have had to contend with being on the sexual predators watch list for the rest of your life."

She started laughing. "Okay, it was sort of funny. But I didn't mean to do that. You have to admit she looked old for her age."

"And by that, if you mean she had ginormous tits, I'll have to agree."

Maddie smacked Carter with a dish towel. "Stop. That's not why I set you two up."

"Oh, so you wanted me to go to jail?"

She furrowed her brow. "No. I wanted you to have some companionship. Sometimes I feel bad that you're such a loner."

"A loner?" Carter had never thought about that. He didn't consider himself much of a loner. Rather, he simply did his thing, and he kept busy, and well, huh. Maybe he was a loner. That sucked. It was like something for losers. And serial killers. Maybe he needed to get out more.

"So, speaking of being a loner, remember I'm still mad at you for that fat-girl remark?"

Carter had pulled the cocktail shaker out of his bag of tricks and started to mix the drinks. "Well, hell. What are you going to make me do now? Bad enough you're trying to set me up with some stranger woman you don't even know—"

"I do so know her."

"Didn't you say she was a new friend or something to that effect?"

"Yeah, but she's perfectly fine and normal. And pretty. You'd be lucky if she agreed to go out with you."

"Thanks for the vote of confidence. But I'm not looking for a relationship right now anyway. I've got too much on my plate. And now Dad's stuff too. Which, by the way, have you had a chance to figure anything out?"

"Stop trying to change the subject. I already told you I have calls in to that clinic he went to along with the oncologist's office. I'm working my way through the HIPPA blockade, and I'm making progress. But it's been baby steps."

"Well, keep me updated on what you find out, please. I may not be the man's biggest fan, but he is my father." Carter gave the cocktail shaker several solid shakes then strained the drinks into the martini glasses, which he'd rimmed with chocolate. He pressed a mint leaf into the chocolate edge of each one. "Voilà. I'm officially off the hook now, right?"

Maddie gave him the side-eye. "Let's see how things play out here tonight and then we'll decide."

"I kind of feel like there needs to be a statute of

limitations on my indebtedness to you."

"Or not." The doorbell rang. "Oooh, I'll get it."

"Be my guest."

Maddie ran to answer the door.

"Jamie!" Maddie gave her new friend a big hug, her bulky hair towel blocking out the girl's face as Carter tried to discreetly get a bead on whether she was either beastly or in middle school.

Maddie looped elbows with Jamie and brought her into the condo.

"Jamie, I've got someone I'd like you to meet."

Chapter Thirteen

NO way. Impossible. It couldn't be. First he's at my work, now he's invaded my friend's world. He's infecting my life like a damned human Ebola virus.

"Jamie, this is my brother, Carter. He's a chef and makes amazing food and he's poured us liquid chocolate bars to drink. Carter, this is my new friend Jamie."

Silence descended on the room.

Maddie looked at Carter, then turned and looked at Jamie, then back again.

"Um, is there a problem?" She looked at one and then the other. "You two know each other already?"

Jamie's mouth spread into a weak-tea sort of smile. "Uhhh—"

"Jamie." Carter came around the bar and reached out his arm to shake her hand. "So lovely to meet you."

Jamie squinted at him, trying to figure out what his game was. "Uh, ye-ahhh."

"I'm so excited for you two to get to know each other. I think you'll hit it off."

Carter took a fast swig of his drink.

"No doubt," he said, a forced smile parting his lips.

Jamie tried hard not to curl her own lip into a snarl. For fuck's sake, this guy had to be her new friend's brother? It couldn't have been anyone else on the planet?

Maddie reached for the towel atop her head. "Omigod, I totally forgot to take this thing off." She held up her finger. "Give me a sec—I'm going to hang this up and drag a comb through my hair."

"Take your time," Jamie said, wishing she could discreetly back up and slip out the front door, never to be missed. The minute her friend disappeared into the bedroom, she threw some shade at Carter.

"Lovely to meet you? Clever."

He shrugged. "I was impressed with my quick thinking," he said, reaching for a drink to hand to her. "I've made our lives infinitely more manageable by not clueing Maddie into the genesis of our relationship."

Jamie rolled her eyes. "I would hardly accuse us of having a relationship."

She heard the blow dryer turn on down the hall and knew they had a few more minutes.

"Besides," Carter said, taking another sip of his drink, "I thought we'd buried the hatchet."

"We did," Jamie said in a quiet hiss. "But it's not as if we're going to date or something. I think your sister was trying to set us up."

"Well, my sister knew that you were a beautiful woman and that I'm a total catch, so she was trying to help out."

"Catch? As in disease?"

Carter laughed. "A sense of humor. I like that."

Jamie squinted. She felt this burning need to be mad at the guy still, but she had agreed to let bygones be bygones, so maybe she should loosen up. "Oh, yeah. I've got a personality as big as my ass."

Carter wagged his finger. "Now, now. We weren't going to go there. Besides, if I didn't say it before, I'll say it now. Men like something to hold on to. Not that I'm saying you have a fat ass, mind you. You don't. It's only that meat versus bones, well, that's a no-brainer."

"Can we stop discussing this? It feels a bit too sexual for me and, well, you'll understand if I never plan to go there with you." Although the thought had crossed her mind that had he not been a jerk to her, he was kind of easy on the eyes. And he clearly had a playful sense of humor. But... no. Just no.

She took a sip of her drink and stopped in her tracks. Her eyes rolled half back in her head. "Oh. My. God." She pointed at the drink. "You made this?"

Carter started to back away. "Did I do something wrong?"

"Wrong?" Jamie opened her eyes again and stared at him. "Are you kidding? This is the most amazing chocolate martini I've ever had. And I've had a few. It's like the mother's milk of chocolate martinis. In fact if mother's milk were like this, well, the world would be a better place."

"And the babies of the world would be perpetually drunk."

She nodded. "There is that, which might not be such a bad thing. Less crying. Dirty diapers wouldn't be such a big deal."

"Babies would probably sleep better, which would mean parents would be well-rested. And that means a happier workplace. Probably eventually fewer wars, even."

She laughed. "Highly confident of you to think your

martini could lead to world peace. Dare I say even arrogant?"

"I like to be an optimist. So you like it?" He smiled. "Which means you like something about me?"

"Don't get too cocky," she said. "Drink's excellent. Still holding out final determinations about the mixologist."

"Mixologist is a regular joe. Likes good food and drink. Pleasant conversation."

"Avoiding controversy."

He shrugged. "Normally, yeah. But once in it, I like to put a stop to it, pronto."

"Brother from another mother! Gimme my drink." Maddie came walking down the hall in fuzzy slippers and an oversized sweatshirt and reached for her cocktail, taking a big slurp. She leaned over and kissed her brother on the cheek. "You are by far my favorite brother, you know."

"I'm your only brother."

"Niggling details."

Carter pointed to her outfit. "Uh, don't let us keep you from heading to bed, Mads."

She held up her hands. "You can't get rid of me that easily, buddy. I'm not going anywhere till you feed me that." She pointed toward the kitchen where the dessert was, then leaned toward Jamie. "Trust me, if you need an excuse to like my brother Carter, that would be it."

Oh, how Jamie wanted to tell her she had plenty of reason to not like the man already. But she was trying to be polite.

"What is this great dessert of salvation, the one that will have us all bowing in supplication to your gifts?"

He shook his head. "I wouldn't go that far. It's good and all, but it's not earth-shattering." He walked over to the kitchen and held up the bowl.

Jamie scrunched her brow. "Huh. It looks like you dropped the bowl on the ground and scooped everything back into it."

"Yeah, but wait'll you taste it," Maddie said as she grabbed three spoons and motioned for her brother to bring it to the living room.

Carter set the large bowl on the coffee table.

"You two, take a seat on the sofa," Maddie said as she plunked down on the floor on the other side of the table. She picked up a spoon. "I'd suggest you grab a spoon and dig in before it's all gone."

Jamie looked at the spoons and then at her friend. "We're eating straight from the bowl?"

"Hell, yes," Carter said. "It's an Eton mess, and there's no other way to eat it than to make a mess."

"Eton mess?" Jamie cocked her head.

"Don't ask. Something to do with the school in England. Supposedly involved a Labrador retriever getting into the dessert. All I know is it's crazy good." He handed her a spoon and stuck his in right as his sister did.

Jamie felt weird doing this but when in Rome… She dug in and pulled up a spoonful of the mixture and opened wide, sliding the concoction past her lips and onto her tongue. She held her breath for a minute.

"Oh, wow." It was cold and sweet and crunchy and smushy and fruity and all-around yummm. "This is freaking fabulous." She stuck her spoon in as the other two did as well.

Carter nodded. "Right?"

"I told you this is my brother's redemption dessert. He even told me he'd done something mean and hurtful to someone and he felt horrible about it. I wasn't quite ready to forgive him for it, but whaddya think, James? Should I forgive him? Is this penance enough?"

Jamie squinted at the two of them. He had told her, hadn't he? And said he felt bad about it? Maybe he truly was repentant about it. Geez, right when she thought she could judge a book by its mean words, here she was having to reevaluate things all over again.

Chapter Fourteen

"THERE'S one thing left in order to grant Carter complete dispensation." Maddie got up for a second to grab her drink.

Carter winced. Here it came. She was going to somehow humiliate him in front of Jamie, when he thought maybe he'd succeeded in pulling the woman off the ledge and making her think maybe he wasn't the world's biggest wanker.

"What could possibly let you forgive him being cruel to a stranger?" Jamie said. She gave Carter a wink.

Maddie looked at her. "How'd you know it was with a stranger?"

Carter came to the rescue. "You said it, you dingbat. You said, and I quote, 'to a complete stranger.'"

"Oh. Sorry. I must've forgotten." She shrugged. "So, here's what could let me forgive him. Drumroll, please." She pounded her fingers on the edge of the cocktail table, then hit one hand in the air at an invisible snare drum. "You, my favoritest brother ever, are going to be my first recruit for the bachelor auction for the women's shelter." She clasped her hands with glee.

"What a brilliant idea!" Jamie nodded. "I think that is a perfect sentence for him after what he did to that poor, defenseless stranger." Carter caught the side-eye she threw his way.

"Well, perhaps I should have made him do my laundry for the next two months. Or fix all my dinners, though I know he has to work, so that wouldn't be too easy. But yeah, I think this will be the redemption I know that deep down in his soul, he seeks."

Carter shook his head, his hands up fending off the threat. "Crap. I'd hoped you'd forgotten about that little death sentence. Seriously, Mads, you can't do that to me. You know how much I hate being the center of attention."

She thrust her lower lip out in a pout. "But, Carter. It's for a good cause. Think of all those women and children who need shelter, and the shelter needs money to help them, and all it takes is a little bit of time out of your life. Think how happy you'd make all those poor victims."

"Not to mention the woman who wins you in the auction." Jamie gave him a wink.

Oooh, so she was digging in the dagger, too, was she? He didn't have half a leg to stand on if she was going to partake in this ploy. This was hardly fair. It was almost as if his sister knew that Jamie was the woman he insulted. God, he'd never want her to know—that would be super mortifying and he'd never live it down. He'd end up being a crotchety old man who she'd still insist on ponying up to be auctioned off when they were old and gray.

Carter looked from Maddie to Jamie and back again. He picked up his drink and threw it back in one gulp. Then he scooped up a fat spoonful of dessert and stuffed it into his mouth. "You're causing me to fall back on my oral fixations by forcing this on me, you know," he said through a mouthful of whipped cream and meringue. The women laughed.

"It won't be so painful, Carter," Maddie said. "You do have to wear a sexy outfit—"

"I'm wearing a snowsuit."

Jamie raised her hand as if she had to ask the teacher permission to go to the girls' room. Maddie called on her.

"I know! I know!" She held up a finger in the air. "Why don't you stipulate that he wear no shirt and he oil his chest?"

What was that saying about how revenge was best served? With malice? With spite? With coldhearted revenge in mind?

He shook his head. "You two are dangerous together," he said, frowning. "I think I'm going to need to be sure to keep you separate before you cause any more damage to my psyche."

"Imagine how good your psyche's going to feel doing penance for being such a cad. Think of it as a less painful sort of punitive hair shirt." Jamie grinned at him as she stuck a spoonful of dessert in her mouth. "After all, when you think of that poor girl you called fat—"

Maddie squinted at her again. "Wait a minute— how'd you know he called a girl fat?"

"You told me that, remember?"

Carter was impressed with how quick she was on her feet. But now was his chance for a little dig. "I don't remember her saying anything about that."

Jamie glared at him. "You weren't here. She mentioned it the other day." She mouthed the words "so there" so Maddie couldn't see it.

Maddie stood up to get drink refills. "Carter—time for round two. We're almost out. Meanwhile, why don't I pull up Netflix and we'll find a movie to watch? Carter, we'll let you pick since you're being such a straight-up guy agreeing to the auction without a fight."

Slight consolation but he'd take what he could get. Maybe he'd pick a terrifying movie, so he could get Jamie to nestle up close to him during the scary parts.

He retreated to the kitchen to fix more martinis while his sister disappeared down the hall and Jamie approached him.

"That's uncharacteristically nice of you to agree to the auction," she said, watching a little too closely as she traced the kitchen tiles with her toes. "I can tell it's something you actively don't want to do, so if I had any sway in that, well, then, thanks."

He shrugged. "If I'd have known it would make you hate me less I'd have done that long ago." They both smiled.

"If it's any consolation, I don't still hate you. At least not totally."

He put his hands over his heart. "Lord have mercy." He gave her a wink. "But seriously, I'm glad we can start over and be friends. And I'd just as soon keep this from her"—he pointed down the hall—"if you're fine with that."

"Not a problem. What happens in the parking lot stays in the parking lot."

He gave himself a mental dope slap, thinking of how many far more enjoyable things he could have done with her in a parking lot instead of his idiot move.

Maddie turned off the lights and they all settled in to watch the film about a couple getting married in a haunted house when the evil spirits take over in the middle of the ceremony and the walls start oozing blood. By the time the walls had started bleeding, Maddie had taken to snoring in the club chair opposite the sofa. Carter ushered her down the hall to her bedroom and tucked her into bed, returning to see Jamie curled up in a fetal position on the sofa.

"This movie is terrifying," she said as he came to sit down and she edged herself closer to him. "I'm never going to be able to sleep tonight!"

Carter extended his arms. "Come here, I'll protect you from the boogeyman. As long as you promise to share the blanket with me." Jamie had staked her claim on the soft blanket at the start of the film at the same time Carter had tried. "And if you honestly don't want to finish it, I'll understand. Though I won't let you live it down that you let a movie get the better of you."

"Oh, no," Jamie said. "I have a hard and fast rule of always finishing what I start. Even if it's a movie that is going to give me nightmares for a week—and don't feel bad about it or anything—I'm going to tough it out."

They resumed watching the movie, with Jamie pressed up against Carter's side, the blanket tucked around their legs. When the bride's face suddenly morphed into a rotting cadaver, Jamie let out a scream and jumped into Carter's arms. He pulled her closer and pressed her face to his chest. "It's okay. It's only a movie. Would you like me to turn it off?"

"I'm not going to chicken out now," she said. "But I wouldn't mind if you'd maybe protect me a little bit?"

She looked up into his eyes, squinting hopefully at him.

He pulled her closer. "It's the least I can do, Jamie." He stared into her eyes and something broke inside him. It was probably about the stupidest thing he could have done besides what he'd done earlier in the week with her, but at least this felt good. Because he pulled her closer so their lips were separated by the slightest hint of air, and then he pressed his to hers, pulling her toward him as he did so.

More than likely, this was going to put him right back in the doghouse with Jamie Lundquist, but he couldn't help himself. He wanted her.

Chapter Fifteen

JAMIE could hardly believe the sudden turn of events. One minute she's afraid some evil spirit is going to penetrate her soul, and the next minute, all she can think about is how much she wants Carter's tongue to penetrate her mouth. And if he wasn't going to make the move, then dammit, she was.

How had she gone from hating this man to horning for him in the blink of an eye? Because right now her sole focus was figuring out how to diplomatically press herself as close to him as possible and hope that he took the hint.

She could hardly believe that she was stretched out on her new friend's sofa, her arms wrapped around Carter's strong shoulders, their lips beginning the delicate dance of sudden attraction. Or was it so sudden? In reality, after she stopped hating him, she'd somehow kept thinking about how adorable it was that a stubborn lock of his blond hair kept insisting on falling in front of those emerald eyes when he was fixated on plating a dish perfectly at work.

And she couldn't help but notice how kind he was to everyone, how interested he was in their lives and their interests. And it had become abundantly clear when she saw him not in those unflattering chef's pants, but rather a worn pair of Levi's, that he had a great ass. She'd be a fool not to take advantage of this position to at least skim her hands down his body and grab a tight hold of him right there, because, well, it was there.

Damn, it had been awhile since she'd had a warm man pressed up against her body and she sure had missed the feeling. So when Carter swept his tongue along the line of her lips, she had no choice but to return the favor, until their tongues met in the middle by happy coincidence as his suddenly roaming hands somehow found her breasts. She moaned into his mouth and he groaned back. She had the presence of mind to think about her actions if only for a fleeting second.

"Are you sure this is such a good idea?" she said as she pressed her hands against his ass, lining him up with her center at exactly the right spot.

"I can't think of a better idea at this very moment. Can you?"

Jamie was too preoccupied to reply.

Their tongues tangled together and she managed to pull his shirt out from the waistband of his jeans, then inch her hands under it, up along his back, enjoying the feeling of corded muscles beneath her palms. Soon his mouth trailed along her jawline, then on to her neck, where he licked and nipped and sucked. Erogenous zone number one for Jamie. Make that two, because soon his tongue led a path along the column of her throat, and, oh God, she needed that. Just. There.

The only thing she needed more was when his hands worked beneath her cashmere sweater and made quick work of her lacy front-closure bra, and then, *heaven!* as his warm hands played with her breasts, measuring the weight of them in his palms first, then finally finding her nipples. And, oh, maybe that was erogenous zone number one because it felt so good, it made Jamie want to straddle the man and ride him to climax.

She was quickly losing count of her favorite erogenous zones when Carter skimmed her sweater over her head, allowing his mouth to continue its trail along the valley of her breasts until finally—finally—his lips found a hard nipple and pulled it into his warm, wet mouth and she about died.

"More," she said as her breathing became rapid, and he obeyed, gently biting her nipple till she gasped in pleasure. She scrambled to pull off his top, then traced her hands over his firm biceps, running her fingers through the light dusting of hair across his chest.

It crossed Jamie's mind that at any minute Maddie could walk in on them, but, nah, she'd had a lot of chocolate martinis, and she was snoring like a grandpa when Carter had put her to bed. Besides, Jamie couldn't stop at this point—she was having far too much fun and it felt… So. Damned. Good.

Carter managed to roll them both so that Jamie was on her back and he was on his side. Thank goodness it was a wide sofa, was all she could think. He practically took her breath away as he continued to play with her nipples with his mouth while his hand stroked along her abdomen. His fingers slipped beneath the edge of her yoga pants and, oh God, right there as his fingers found their way under the edge of her panties. They slid between her lips and he traced a slick trail around her center as she let out a loud groan. To think she believed she could be satisfied with dessert and chocolate martinis.

She was completely bare. Full Monty. And it felt so good. And smooth. And wet. That's all the information Carter could process once he got past the idea that he was seriously feeling up Jamie Lundquist on his sister's sofa. He could hardly figure out where to begin once he'd placed his lips on hers but thank goodness muscle memory kicked in.

It had been so long he was worried he'd have forgotten, but nah, he still knew his way around a woman's body, and this body, well, it was making him particularly happy. Her tits fit his palms perfectly, so soft and heavy and suckable, and those nipples—it's as if they were made to be pulled tightly into his mouth. He about came in his pants when she demanded more of him, and he happily obliged, biting down on one nipple until she shouted out in pleasure.

Tonight, her pleasure was his only goal. He wanted nothing more than to make it all up to her the best way he knew how: by bringing her to a heaving, moaning, panting orgasm. Or two. Or three.

Carter drew his attention to the hard nipple pressed up against his warm tongue as he bathed it in moisture. He was lucky; as a chef, he had no choice but to multitask, and that came in mighty handy when it came to women. He was perfectly capable of sucking hard on her tits while his fingers made fast work of her pussy, slipping easily between the folds as her breath became more rapid and her moans more frequent. He didn't even have to ask her to spread her legs because she'd readily parted them wide to allow him easy access. He figured that meant he could fully pay her back for his untoward behavior.

So he inched his way downward, his tongue trailing along her belly then lower, where he flattened his tongue and gave a long, slow lick once he reached her bare pussy and that perfect, swollen clit. He spread her lips and slid first one, then another finger inside her, her juices coating his fingers as he lapped at them along the seam of her body. Jamie thrust her hips toward his mouth, encouraging him, as his mouth met her moist core and his tongue danced around her clit, his fingers rhythmically working their way in and out of her wet center. She combed her fingers through his hair, pressing his face to her, encouraging him on, her hip thrusts coming harder and faster. Carter reached up and pinched a nipple hard as he thrust his fingers into her, working his tongue long and slow along her till she finally broke, her body tensing before she shouted out his name as she rode his face to climax.

He hoped she didn't think they were done. After all, he was only getting started.

Chapter Sixteen

JAMIE had always been taught to not play with her food, but damn, when Carter at some point spread that crazy-good dessert he'd made along her nipples and sucked and licked it off, well, she knew that had always been a bad piece of advice. Clearly whoever had decided that hadn't had the distinct pleasure of having food licked off of erogenous zones number one, two, three, four, and five.

For that matter, Jamie was finding pleasure points she never knew existed. The damnedest thing is that Carter wouldn't let her return the favor. Try as she might, he kept telling her it was all about her. And, far be it from her to argue with him. Ahem. Of course she knew somewhere in the reptilian part of her brain that she was going to have to reconcile herself with what was and what is, come sunrise, but for now, well, wow.

Somewhere in the middle of the night, the two of them passed out on Maddie's sofa, too tired to move. At least they had the presence of mind to remember to put their clothes back on in case Maddie surprised them. Jamie woke up somewhere around five in the morning and took one look at Carter and knew she had to get the hell out of that apartment before morning slapped her in the face. Sure, she'd had a fantastic time, and ya-freaking-hoo for it. She'd had more male-induced orgasms in three hours than she'd had in the past nine months and evidently she needed that. But she wasn't quite sure what this all meant and she sure as hell didn't want to have to figure that out on the spot with Maddie—not to mention Carter—in the morning. Awkward!

She slipped her boots back on, grabbed her coat and purse, and tiptoed ever so quietly out the front door. A light coating of snow had fallen overnight, and she had to take caution to not wipe out on the steps on the way down. How embarrassing would that be, her pulling a runner, only to have Carter find her splayed out, unable to move, on the steps in an hour or so. She had a half a mind to divert to the gym on her way home, but one swipe under her eyes revealed a crust of mascara and last night's makeup on her fingertips, and she knew she'd be a dead giveaway for being on a walk-o-shame workout. In any case, it was too risky. She might run into him there, and, well, enough said. She was off tonight, so could avoid encountering Carter for at least this evening. Besides, at work, there would be no way to have that discussion. She was happy to put this confrontation off as long as possible. Call her a wimp, but oh well.

"Good morning, glory," Maddie said as she padded into the kitchen and started to put the coffee on.

Carter had woken up a few minutes earlier, only to realize Cinderella had pulled a runner, not even leaving a glass slipper behind. Dammit. And here he thought he'd made such good headway. At least he knew for sure he'd given good head. He half groaned in response to his sister.

"Where's Jamie?"

"Uh, she left last night. After you fell asleep."

Maddie thrust out her lower lip. "Well, rats. I'm sorry I was the party pooper. I was so hoping you two would hit it off. I didn't want my going to bed to end all the fun."

Carter thought back to a few hours ago when he was licking dessert off of Jamie's delectable pussy, and he smiled.

"No worries. We had plenty of fun."

"Oh, too bad I forgot to put the dessert away," she said, grabbing the bowl from the kitchen counter and putting it in the sink to soak.

"I think we enjoyed that sweet treat plenty." He smiled to himself. Oh, yeah.

Maddie set Carter's coffee on the counter, then opened the dishwasher and started unloading dishes.

"So what'd you think?"

Carter turned toward his sister. "Of?"

"Of Jamie, of course."

He shrugged. "She seemed nice. Why?"

"Why? Are you kidding me?" She walked toward her brother and swatted him with a dishtowel. "Why don't you ask her out?"

"I'm kinda busy with work, ya know?"

"You, my brother, need to get laid."

"So you're pimping out your friends now?"

She hit him again with the towel. "Stop! It's only she seems sweet and she's super cute, and I'm trying to help you find a distraction other than work. All work makes Carter a cranky boy."

"I don't know if she even liked me." Carter took a sip of his coffee.

"Why don't you take a chance and see. Go ahead and ask her out. Ask her to coffee. It's not like you have to ask her to sleep with you on the first date." Carter choked and spat out his drink.

"Carter! All over my white carpet!"

He held up his hands. "Oh, man, I'm so sorry, Mads. I really didn't mean to do that. Here, let me clean it up." He grabbed her dishtowel, wet it, and wiped up his splattered coffee.

"Just for that, you have to promise me you'll try."

"Try what?"

"Try to ask her out. Please? I think you both could use the distraction. Deal?" She scribbled Jamie's phone number on a scrap of paper and handed it to him.

Carter heaved a sigh as he took the paper. "All right. Fine. I'll see."

Chapter Seventeen

JAMIE passed canapés to guests arriving at the restaurant's official introductory event for Carter. It was her first time back at work since her unexpected dalliance with him on Sunday night. She was grateful she could totally dodge his attention tonight, as he would be pulled in all sorts of directions for the rest of the evening. It took the monkey off her back for one more day.

Carter had left several messages on her cell phone, and repeated texts as well. She ignored them all, which she knew was a bit lame, but she was so conflicted about all this. Part of her found it hard to shake that initial impression of the man, even though she had forgiven him. And another part of her was kind of embarrassed she had done what she'd done out of nowhere. One minute they were watching a movie and the next, his mouth was on her breast, and she loved it. Wow, had she loved it. That man sure knew his way around a woman's body.

Which brought her to the part of her that wanted a command performance. But that was a terrible idea. For one thing, they worked together. It was never good to muck that up with sex. And then she had only recently started being friends with his sister. That was always a recipe for disaster, having surreptitious sex with a friend's sibling. Something eventually had to give there.

Jamie looked up to see her least favorite person strut through the door like she was the queen of Sheba. Jennifer Lorenzini, a reporter for WVBH-TV. Jennifer loved to take swipes at Jamie, for reasons Jamie had yet to figure out. Tall with long, wavy black hair, Jennifer was a striking presence wherever she showed up, and she knew it. Maybe she hated that Jamie remembered her when she was an ugly, pimply-faced tween who had the personality of a garbage bin. Sure, she was beautiful now, damn her, but her personality hadn't changed much.

Jamie's father grabbed Jennifer's hand and led her right to Carter to make introductions. This was where Jamie felt sort of demeaned, subserviently offering up appetizers while the "grown-ups" socialized. Or at least that's what it felt like. She worked the crowd on the periphery of Carter and Jennifer, trying to home in on their conversation.

"Oooh, Frank, you certainly know how to pick them," Jennifer was saying as she held Carter's hand a beat too long. "So tall and blond and handsome."

Carter squinted at her. "I'd like to believe he hired me based on my cooking skills."

She elbowed him in the ribs. "I'd love to see what you might cook up for me."

Jamie wanted to smack her. And she was sorely tempted to grab a tray of drinks and trip and spill it all over Jennifer's winter-white wool suit. Who wears winter-white wool anymore? Seriously. Instead she wedged herself between Carter and Jennifer with a tray of shrimp cakes. Jamie stood behind Jennifer and stuck her finger in her mouth like she was trying to throw up.

"Jamie! What a surprise to see you here. You still doing Nick and Tony?" She held up her pointer and middle fingers and twisted them like two lovers entangled.

Jamie glared at her, but Jennifer wasn't done.

"Jamie here, not to be satisfied with one guy, decided to take on two at a time. Amiright, James?"

Jamie was glad her father had migrated over toward another conversation, so he wasn't privy to the beyotch trying to make her look bad. Not that he was in the dark about Jamie's romantic interludes—he'd met both men along the way. She hadn't kept either of them a secret, not from each other or anyone else. But the way Jennifer was portraying it made Jamie sound so slutty.

So she'd dated two guys at the same time. What was the big deal with that? And so if she decided she wanted to sleep with them in the course of their dating period, why was that so criminal?

"You probably don't want to make your halitosis problem worse by eating these shrimp cakes, eh, Jennifer?" Jamie knew her father would kill her for stooping to such a comment, but sometimes a girl had to do what a girl had to do.

Carter glared at Jamie then turned away from her, putting his hand on the reporter's shoulder, moving her away from the conversation.

Fine, let him do that. For all she cared, let him discover for himself about Jennifer Lorenzini's bad breath. Jamie could care less.

Carter wasn't about to let this one go. He was determined to get face time with Jamie to figure out where he stood. And with her behavior tonight, he was left all the more mystified. Before she could slip out, he took the liberty of doing so and leaned against the driver's side door of her car as she walked to the parking lot.

"Carter?"

"None other." He crossed his arms over his chest.

"You need something?"

He arched an eyebrow. "That's a loaded question."

"Okay, well, I'm tired and need to get home." She held her key fob toward him, motioning she wanted to get into her car.

"What was up with you in there?" He aimed his thumb toward the restaurant.

She wrinkled her brow. "What? I helped to set up. I served appetizers. I cleaned up afterward."

"And that reporter in there?" He nodded toward the door.

Jamie rolled her eyes. "She's such a bitch. I dated a guy she wanted to date about a lifetime ago. Ever since then, she's been mean to me."

"Hence the comments about the two guys?"

Jamie crossed her arms over her chest. "What about

them?"

"So you had two lovers at the same time?"

She grinned. "That sounds sort of sordid when you say it like that. Did I date two men at the same time? Quasi-seriously? Yes."

"And you were sleeping with them both?"

"Am I under arrest here? What's with the police interrogation?"

Carter threaded his fingers through his hair. "Because I'm trying to understand who Jamie Lundquist is."

"What's it your business?"

"Because I like you, Jamie. I find you to be an extremely compelling woman. Fun to spend time with. Not to mention I think you're beautiful, I had an amazing time with you, and I'd love to try for a command performance."

"But because I was having sex with two different men over the course of several months, that disqualifies me?"

He shook his head. "I didn't say anything of the sort. To be honest, I don't like to think of you sleeping with any other men. I mean you and I haven't even 'officially' slept together." He made air quotes around the word. "So since I haven't yet had that pleasure, I certainly don't feel all warm inside imagining you with not one man but two." He leaned toward her, then winced. "Please tell me it wasn't at the same time."

Jamie glared at him. "So what if it was?"

"Seriously? You had sex with them both at the same time?"

"Don't be an idiot, Carter," she said. "The answer to

your question is no, but the bigger answer to your question is so what? It would be perfectly fine for you to sleep with two women at the same time, right? I'm sure you've done it. It's every guy's holy grail. So why would it matter if I did the same thing? The fact is, I liked both guys. They each had their strong points. Sexually, as well. Nick, well, my God." Her eyes grew large. "Let's just say size matters."

It was Carter's turn to roll his eyes. He knew he sized up pretty damn well, and that was something Jamie had yet to discover.

"And Toby, he had this trick with his tongue that sent me into a frenzy."

Carter gave her one of those "come off it" looks. "I'm pretty sure I was able to do that, with or without the special effects."

"My point is, it's okay for a guy to double dip, even quadruple dip, but God forbid a woman take her consensual sexual pleasure with a variety of partners, without judgment from some asshole who already showed what a judgmental prick he could be." She no sooner said it than she covered her mouth with her hand.

Carter reached for Jamie's hand. "Look, Jamie. I'm going to pretend you didn't say that because I don't want to derail things here. This conversation has gone offtrack. I'm not here to grill you about your past sexual exploits. I simply wanted to tell you I had a lot of fun with you the other night. And I'd love to get to know you better. Can I take you out on a real date, maybe?"

She paced in front of him, not saying a word. He watched intently as the steam of her breath snaked through the night air while she continued not to answer him. "I don't know, Carter. I need some time to think about it." She turned to look at him. "Besides, it looks like Jennifer has it bad for you. Maybe you should pursue her. She could give you lots of great publicity, which I'm sure is all you want anyhow. But look out—her breath is the worst."

Jamie turned to walk away from Carter, so he let her. He was going to have to figure out another way to skin this cat, and he would. He'd figure it out one way or another.

Chapter Eighteen

"ARE you ready to tell me what bee has flown up your ass, Jamie?"

Jamie's friend Cameron Sanders had met her for drinks. The two had been close friends since childhood and minced no bullshit between them.

Jamie sighed. "I don't know, Cam. These past many months have been so messed up. My parents have yanked me around so much, I honestly don't even know who to believe anymore. They butter me up so that I'll side with them. My dad sleeps with someone young enough to be his daughter. My mother's talking about hooking up with men half her age. And I'm flapping in the wind, waiting tables, not doing any art, eating myself into double-digit dress sizes."

Cam held open his hands and gave his friend a big hug. "Crap, James. I'm sorry you've been going through this. And I'm so sorry I haven't been paying much attention. I guess I've been busy with the bar, and well, Lacy and stuff."

Just as things were imploding in Jamie's world, Cameron had all sorts of exciting new things happen, including inheriting a local landmark—a mermaid cocktail lounge—and falling in love with one of the mermaids. Jamie was thrilled for Cameron, but she did miss these little heart-to-hearts they used to have often.

"I feel like there's something else you're not telling me."

Jamie took a swig of her wine. "What are you—the soothsayer or something?"

"I can tell. Talk to your friend, Cam. Let it all out."

"Fine. There's this guy."

He slapped the bar. "I knew it!"

"How did you know it?"

"Because I do."

"You're being weird."

"You have this weird glow about you. It's kind of an angry glow, like a radioactive missile, but nonetheless, it's a glow. Tell me about him."

"What if I'm kind of embarrassed to?"

"Don't be ridiculous. I've literally thrown up on you before. That's about as embarrassing as it gets. So spare me that nonsense." The two had shared plenty of embarrassing life experiences over the years, and she knew it was silly to stonewall him at this point.

"All right, here goes. I encountered this guy who was super mean to me and called me fat. It turns out he works for my dad and he felt awful about being a jerk and apologized a whole lot. Then I made friends with this girl and dammit, he happens to be her brother, so I had to be nice to him when she invited me to her house. We got kind of drunk and next thing you know, we made out and, well, more than made out—"

"You made out with your new friend?"

She shook her head hard. "Of course not. I don't go that way."

"Oh, so you made out with the brother who insulted you?"

"After he apologized about a thousand times. And he makes such good chocolate martinis. And desserts too. And maybe we did a little more than make out."

"You slept with him?"

"No! I didn't sleep with him. I mean we didn't do *it* if that's what you're asking."

"Ahh, I see. Everything but the kitchen sink."

She shook her head. "Not even everything. In fact, I did nothing to him. Or for him. How do you guys prefer to refer to that?"

"So he did you but not vice versa?"

"I'm trying to tell you he wouldn't let me. He was trying to make it up to me I think, like let it all be about me."

"First off, James, that's the most selfless act a man can confer upon another human being. Secondly, sounds like he succeeded."

She rolled her eyes. "Beyond his wildest dreams."

"So you're dating him now?"

"No."

"Why the hell not?"

"It's complicated."

Cameron pretended to slap her across the face a couple of times. "Are you mad, woman? You've got a guy who focuses on you, cooks up a case of blue balls to please you, he likes you so much, and yet you're snubbing him?"

"But we work together. And I'm fat. And everything's so messed up in my life."

Cameron reached for her hands and wrapped his

around them. "I'm gonna talk friend to friend here. And I want you to listen. Are you listening?"

She nodded as she sipped her wine.

"Stop fucking overthinking everything, Jamie. Look." He brushed her hair behind her ear. "We've known each other a long, long time. And I'm not gonna lie: for a long time, you lived a charmed life. Happily married parents. Great home. Great life. Pampered only child. But then things took a turn. And life's like that. It's not always going to be easy. So you need to figure out how to weather the storms and not let them sink you. This won't be the only time in your life that things will be tough. But it certainly will inform everyone else about whether you're willing to man up and make lemonade out of lemons. To mix metaphors."

"So what're you telling me?"

"I'm telling you to go reward the guy with a blow job. And maybe while you're at it, show him what an easy lay you are." He leaned over and poked his elbow into her ribs. "And I'm telling you this because I love you. Go, be fruitful and multiply."

She smacked his arm. "You are such a weirdo. I am not going to be fruitful, that's for damned sure."

"But the rest? You'll at least think about it?"

She propped her elbow on the bar and leaned forward. "Okay, I will. But honestly, only because it's been days since we last, er, um, and I'm kind of itching for round two."

Jamie got up to go to the bathroom and as she turned a corner in the bar, she overhead familiar voices. She turned to see her mother and father laughing and drinking, their hands clasped together like they actually liked each other. What the fuck? She tucked away into the shadows, trying to hear their conversation.

"Honestly, Frankie, whatever were you thinking?"

"I'm sorry, Leslie, I was an ass. Will you ever forgive me?"

"Trust me, babe, you're going to be paying for this for a long, long time."

"Would a trip to the Caribbean help?"

"It's a start. A meager one, but a start."

Her father flagged the waiter. "A bottle of your finest champagne."

At that, Jamie ducked away to the bathroom and took the long way around the restaurant back to the bar up front afterward.

"You're not even going to believe what I overheard," she said, shaking her head.

"A dancing hippo?"

"More like a groveling ass."

Cam leaned on his elbows, his chin resting on his hands. "Do tell."

"My father. Apologizing to my mother. Offering a trip to the Caribbean to make amends."

Cameron slapped his thigh. "See, like I said. Life is filled with ups and downs, and you never know what the hell's gonna happen next. Here you went from DEFCON 2 to détente, maybe even peace accords. For all you know, hell could freeze over tomorrow."

She rolled her eyes. "Trust me, hell has officially frozen over."

"In that case, call that hot lead of yours and pick up where you left off before it's too late."

"One last bit of nooky before it all goes to hell? I

suppose you've got a point."

Of course Jamie didn't want to utter the words out loud, but she was craving Carter Henderson. And that scared the ever-loving shit out of her.

Chapter Nineteen

"WHAT do you mean Dad doesn't have lung cancer?" Carter was talking to his sister on the phone on his way home from the gym—where, yet again, there was no sign of Jamie, dammit.

"Well he's got a tumor, but it's benign."

"So like he's not going to die?"

"Of course he's going to die."

"But I thought you said he was okay." Carter flicked his turn indicator, en route for coffee and doughnuts.

"Carter, everyone's going to die."

Carter scrubbed his face with his hand. Did he have to be completely literal with everything? "I mean he's not going to die from this tumor in his lungs?"

"No. The doctor said they weren't even going to do anything about it. They're going to wait and see. Often they get reabsorbed into the tissue. But she did want to be sure his pneumonia was all gone."

"He's got pneumonia?"

"Didn't you notice that rattling sound when he was breathing? And that phlegmy cough where it sounded like he was spewing out a lung?"

"To be honest, I haven't been there but for the day I dropped off the soup. I've been swamped with work."

"So, yeah, he's got pneumonia. But he's getting better. I'm sure your soup was therapeutic. Why don't you make some more for him?"

"I'll get right on it. In the meantime, I'm gonna grab a doughnut. Thanks for staying on that and I guess we should be deeply relieved."

"I know you are deep down, Carter. It's hard for you. I get that. Don't beat yourself up over it, okay?"

He'd pulled up in front of the doughnut shop, happy the daily line hadn't formed yet. All he wanted was to grab breakfast on the go and get home to work on the books for the woman who owned the dance studio. He had a long day ahead of him.

"So any luck with Jamie?"

"Nope. She's as elusive as a dodo bird."

"Aren't they extinct?"

He sighed. "Yep. Pretty sure she is too. At least when it comes to me."

"Take heart, big brother. You never know what your day could bring you."

"I'll settle for a doughnut and a cup of coffee. Love you, Mad Maddie!"

"Don't give anyone food poisoning at work today!"

"Thanks. I'll try my hardest."

Carter was busy checking messages on his phone and didn't even notice till he bumped into someone who was heading into the doughnut shop ahead of him.

"Oh, man, I'm so sorry," he said as he looked down to see Jamie standing there. If he were honest, he'd say she looked like a squirrel that didn't know which way to run on the highway before the truck splattered her. "Jamie?"

"Hey, Carter. How's it going?"

He nodded. "It's going. You?"

"Look. I've wanted to reach out to you."

"Funny, that. Because I wanted to reach out to you, too. Well, I did in fact, but it backfired."

"About that—"

"Honestly, you don't owe me any apologies, Jamie. If you aren't interested in me, I'll live. It's a little bit of an ego blow after I thought I'd worked my magic on you, but I know someday there will be a woman who will settle for me and it'll all be fine and good."

They stepped up to the counter.

"Breakfast is on me—what'll it be?" Jamie asked.

"Ah, big spender. In that case, I'll get three glazed doughnuts and a tall coffee, black."

"Three? I hate how men can scarf down as many doughnuts as their hearts desire and never pay the price for it."

"Trust me, it's not even worth the sacrifice. I mean they taste good, but after a few bites, you don't even taste them anymore. It's more like filling for your gut, you know?"

She ordered for them both, and after picking up their orders walked outside.

"Can I drop you someplace?" Carter asked.

"I can walk—I live right around the corner."

"Hop in. It's the least I can do after you splurged on breakfast for me."

He unlocked the door and opened it for her, helped boost her up and in, then handed up the coffee to her.

He hopped in his side and started the engine.

"So this is the infamous SUV, huh?" She ran her

hand along the dashboard. "The one so big you have to take up two spaces."

"Look out, or you might find yourself wearing your coffee."

She turned to face him. "You wouldn't do that to me, would you?"

"Not deliberately, but there are an awful lot of potholes on the road between here and your place."

"You don't even know where my place is."

He shrugged. "You got me. Show me the way."

She directed him to turn down toward the ocean road, and they drove about a quarter of a mile till they came to her cottage.

"Cute place," he said as he parked the car. "You gonna invite me in?"

"Well, you could wait till I asked you rather than making it seem as if you invited yourself."

"Just wanted to put undue pressure on you so you felt bad."

"Mission accomplished." She grinned at him. "Actually, mission not accomplished. I'd like to extend an offer for you to join me as I dine on my healthful and nutritional doughnut-and-coffee breakfast in the comfort of my own home."

"I thought you'd never ask."

Carter got out and opened the car door for her, helping her down, then followed her into her place."

"Impressive property for someone on a waitress budget."

"Paid for in blood money, thanks," she said. "My father trying to woo me after banging the maid. He wanted me to still like him even if my mother hated him."

"How'd that work for him?"

"Pretty miserably."

"Parent bullshit... It's such crap, isn't it?"

She held up her hands in surrender. "Tell me about it. So much crap, and then when you're not looking, they turn around and get back together. And don't even freaking tell you about it. You have to learn about it by eavesdropping in dark restaurants."

He lifted a brow as he pulled up a seat on the sofa. "Detective work?"

"Bathroom stop."

"Okay, then."

"I was at a bar, went to pee, happened to see my father wooing my mother and whispering sweet nothings into her ear on my way to the ladies' room."

"I guess it's better than running into them fighting?"

"You've got a point there. Seen enough of that to last a lifetime."

"I hear ya. I saw enough crap with my parents to know what I didn't ever want in my life."

Jamie took a bite of her doughnut, washing it back with a swig of coffee. "What's that?"

"A serious relationship. Nothing good ever comes of that. Then you get bogged down. Things get shitty. You're stuck with kids. Someone leaves, then it's all fucked up forever."

"Well, aren't we cheery this fine morning?"

Carter stuffed a fat bit of doughnut into his mouth. "What can I say? It's all I've ever known. Maddie says I need to get my shit together and stop dwelling on the past."

"Maddie sounds like a wise woman."

"Except I decided to take a chance on that and it backfired."

Jamie pursed her lips. "I'm sorry. That's all on me."

He shook his head. "It's okay, though. Really. Because it served as a reminder that relationships and I don't seem compatible. I couldn't even keep my mom around, you know? So how could I ever expect a woman to stick around?"

"Your mom left you?"

He nodded. "Yup. I guess mothering wasn't her scene. She filled a suitcase one day and walked out the door. It broke my father. He never did recover from it. And it stuck me with her duties—I had to be the mom, the dad, the everything. Since then, my father could never quite get his shit together. He always flounders with get-rich-quick schemes that fail, and I'm always there to catch him when he falls. But these were good lessons to learn. Don't get too close to someone. It's much safer that way."

"Let me ask you something." Jamie turned to face him on the sofa. He nodded his assent. "Why do you have to keep on catching your father? He's a grown man, Carter. He's got to sink or swim on his own. You have your life to live. Isn't it time you left him to figure out how to live his? Cause you can't fix it for him, you know. He's the only one who's ever going to be able to do that."

"I suppose you're right." He sighed. "But it's hard, watching him fail time and again."

"But your interventions haven't helped him not to fail, have they?"

He shook his head. "So, then maybe it's just as well to let it go and see what happens."

"Where'd you get so smart?"

"It's always easier analyzing someone else's problems than it is your own."

"In that case, how about I try my hand with yours?"

Chapter Twenty

"SO why did you leave my phone calls and text messages unanswered?" Carter had set down his coffee and licked the remaining sugar from his fingertips before he leaned forward on both hands, his face right up to Jamie's.

"Because I'm a chickenshit?" Jamie figured if he had the courage to bare his soul a bit, it was the least she could do in return.

"Chickenshit because you didn't like me? Or because you were afraid you did?"

"Because you scared the crap out of me, is why."

"But I'm just a big ole teddy bear," he said, his hands slowly creeping toward her.

"Who's so freaking good with his mouth, it should be illegal," she said. She thought about that and her heart started to race in her chest. What the hell had she been thinking not encouraging more of *that*? Must be temporary insanity of some sort.

"Aha… So you did like it?"

She blinked. "Are you kidding me? Any woman who didn't like that would need to have her head examined."

"Was I as good as—was that Toby with the magical tongue?"

She laughed. He remembered his name? "Trust me,

you were Toby on steroids."

"So then why wouldn't you have come back for more?" he said, his hands reaching for her hair. "I know if I had experienced a magical mouth on my cock, I'd have been demanding a command performance at least once a day."

"But you wouldn't even let me go there."

He ran his fingers through her hair, tucking strands behind her ears. She loved the soothing feel of it.

"Because I wanted to pleasure you. It wasn't about me."

Carter took the coffee cup out of Jamie's hand and set it on the coffee table. Then he removed his jacket, tossing it over the back of the sofa. He unzipped her down vest next, casting it alongside his jacket. Jamie closed her eyes, bracing herself for what was to come.

"If we are going to try to recreate what happened between us, this time you have to promise I get to have my way with you, too."

"Be my guest," he said, pulling her onto his lap as he wrapped his arms around her and settled his lips over hers.

Jamie couldn't believe her good fortune of running into him this morning. Here she'd been wanting to muster up the courage to apologize to him and maybe see where things might go, but she'd been a coward all week long. Every time she'd walked into the kitchen this past week, she'd stared at him, wanting to come up behind him and wrap her arms around his waist and slide her fingers below the waistband of his pants to find his cock hard and waiting for her. But there were always people around. And that would have been verboten at work, anyhow.

And now here she was, nestled in his lap, her body pressed up against that very hard cock she had been fantasizing about for days.

"Would it be forward of me to want to dry hump your cock until I came?" She dragged her tongue along his lips.

"No more forward than me wanting to pull down your yoga pants and slide that cock into your wet pussy."

Jamie's hips had already started moving of their own volition, rubbing up and back across him. They both moaned.

"In which case, you won't mind too terribly if I remove your shirt?"

"As long as you don't mind if I slip yours over your head, along with that all-too-confining sports bra." He pulled her top off. "Ah, but zip front. Brilliant invention." He slid it down and her breasts immediately spilled out from their confines.

"Would it be rude of me to ask you to suck on my nipples the way you did the other night? Because that got me crazy wet, and I think you'll probably want me wet for what we're going to do."

"Please tell me you have condoms."

"Please tell me you fit an XL."

"Please help me get these pants off of you before I explode on you." Carter toed off his sneakers and socks and shifted his shorts off as she pulled hers down till finally they were both naked. Jamie straddled Carter's lap as she stroked and admired his most admirable cock.

"Very nice, Mr. Henderson. I think this will do fine."

He reached down and dragged the tip of his cock

along her folds.

"You don't mind if we dispense with formalities? I say we cut to the chase now and then we can get back to all the other good stuff afterward. I've been dying to slide my cock into you and I won't be satisfied until I do."

She stood quickly and grabbed his hand, pulling him toward the bedroom. "Condoms. There. Now." They raced down the hall and into her bedroom, and she pushed him back on the bed and reached into her nightstand drawer for a condom. In no time, she tore it with her teeth and carefully placed it over his swollen head, rolling it down his length, then again spread her legs over his hips, easing herself onto his cock slowly. She gasped in pleasure as he groaned.

Once she was seated all the way onto him, she rolled her hips, letting him slide from her depths, only to plunge back down onto him.

"You're fucking killing me," he said, watching her through slitted eyes.

"Your mouth looks like it needs something to do," she said, leaning over so that he could take a nipple into her mouth. He reached around and pressed his fingers to the place where their bodies met and he added a finger. They both moaned.

Jamie picked up the pace, lifting off his cock long enough to plunge back down. Carter held tight to her hips for better leverage while he took turns nipping and licking and sucking her nipples.

"I'm close, Jamie," he said, slipping a finger between them, slicking it along her lips and circling her clit. "Come for me, baby." She let out a shout as stars burst behind her eyelids, tremors of release bolting through her body as he pumped hard then stiffened, his cock seated deep inside her as he released.

She fell on top of him, their sweaty bodies slicked together as their heavy breaths comingled. For a second, she was grateful that she'd probably burned off at least one of the doughnuts she shouldn't have eaten for breakfast. But then she was even more pleased that she'd had the best-ever makeup sex with a man she hadn't been sure how to make up with in the first place. She should've known sex was the best way to do that.

Chapter Twenty-One

WELL, this was the kind of bookkeeping he'd opt for hands down. Because that had originally been the only thing on his agenda this morning: bookkeeping and nothing else. Instead he found himself with his cock buried balls-deep inside the woman who had been vexing him for the past few weeks and he couldn't be happier. Fuck accounting. He could do this with her all day long and life would be perfect.

Perfect. Yes. No doubt of that when Jamie scooted down his torso and, wrapping her fist around his cock, licked his cock like a lollipop. Had he died and gone to heaven? He fixed his focus on her tongue as it dragged along the quickly swelling head of his cock, then worked its way around the rim. And when she paused, her tongue pressed to him in such an intimate way, and looked into his eyes, life didn't get any better than that.

It wasn't long before Jamie took his dick into her mouth, her lips slowly pulling him inward, her tongue pressed along the length while she sucked hard. Carter tucked her hair behind her ears so he could get a better view as he greedily thrust his hips toward her mouth. And he was close to going off as she squeezed his balls and sucked him in. He tugged on her, but she shook her head.

"I'm close, James," he said. "And I want to come inside of you."

"My mouth is inside of me," she said, pausing from her task.

"But I want to be in your warm, wet pussy. Now come here."

He pulled her toward him.

"How do you want it?" he said, wrestling with the many ways he wanted to take her.

"How do *you* want it?" She threw him a coy look.

"On your hands and knees." He used his hands to direct her.

"My thoughts exactly," she said as she posed for him on all fours, looking over her shoulder as he sheathed himself and slid inside her.

"Fuck, Jamie, you're killing me," he said as he pressed himself deep inside.

"Can't think of a better way to go." She grinned as she arched her back, moving her body toward his to meet him all the way.

Carter curled his body over her as he began to pump in earnest in hard thrusts, Jamie meeting him each time his cock speared her. He reached beneath her, his fingers sliding along her wet folds to play with her swollen clit.

"Come for me, Jamie," he said, his breathing hard and fast. "I want to feel your pussy squeeze the come out of me."

He increased the pace of his fingers playing with her sex, circling her clit, gathering moisture from her opening and spreading it over her lips.

"Oh, Carter," she said on a moan. "I'm about to

come all over your hard cock. Bury it deep in me now."

He could feel the spasms rippling through her pussy in powerful waves as it pulled on his dick. His own orgasm hit hard, his seed spurting in a seemingly endless stream as his body convulsed with pleasure.

He collapsed on top of her, still inside her, sweaty and exhausted and amazingly satisfied.

Later, Jamie lay with her head on Carter's chest. Her fingers traced lazy swirls along his chest, then followed the happy trail of hair that led from his navel to the holy grail, then back up again.

"Carter?"

"Uh-huh," he said, his voice quiet and low. They'd drifted off to sleep a few times over the past few hours, and Jamie knew they both needed to get going soon so they could get ready for work.

"Did you mean what you said earlier?"

He opened an eye and looked down at her. "When I said you were the most unbelievably fuckable woman I've ever been with?"

She shook her head. "You probably say that to all the ladies."

"Believe me when I say I haven't."

"I mean what you said earlier when we were talking."

"When our mouths were talking before our bodies took over doing all the talking?"

She nodded. "Yeah."

"What part are you referring to?"

"When you said you'd never be in a relationship. Because of your parents."

He took a deep breath. "I don't believe in commitment. Or maybe by that I mean I don't have faith in it. So if I don't trust commitment, then it would be wrong of me to lie to anyone and say I could."

Jamie was silent for a few minutes.

He ran his fingers through her hair.

"You got something to say about that?" he said.

She shook her head as disappointment washed over her. She'd been such an idiot to think it was a good idea to give of herself to this guy. She should have trusted her gut—she loved a good fuck like the next girl, but today was different. Or at least it seemed different. She thought he had started to have real feelings for her. And she certainly had them for him.

But obviously, pretending this thing happening between them would be more than mutual sexual gratification was a waste of her time. And that was fine in a relationship if that's what both partners wanted. But she'd tricked herself into thinking that maybe there was something more there, something that could develop into a real relationship. It made her sad to think what maybe could be, under other circumstances.

A tiny tear found its way to the corner of her eye, and she quickly swiped it away.

"Nope. Nothing at all." She rolled off of him. "Well, that was fun. Great sex. I appreciate the orgasms, but I've gotta shower and get ready for work." She reached for a T-shirt on the chair next to her bed and pulled it on to cover herself. It felt better to have some sort of physical shield between them. "Oh, and this thing?" She motioned between them with her finger. "Let's keep it on the down low, okay? I don't want anyone at work to know that we did this. It would look bad, plus then people might start thinking there was something more than it is. K?"

Carter stared at her.

"And I'm sure you can find your way out. Thanks. This was, uh, fun."

Chapter Twenty-Two

THIS was, uh, fun? What the fuck did she mean by that? Jesus. Chicks. One minute they're happily sucking your cock; the next minute they're acting all wounded and mysterious as if you'd beaten them with it. Carter could never figure them out. All the more reason he never, ever wanted to be in a serious relationship with one. Hell, he'd spend his days having to decipher their moods and their words and intentions. It was hard enough figuring out his own intentions.

If he gave it some serious thought, he'd realize what was at the root of that cold front that had swept through her bedroom thirty minutes ago like a damned nor'easter, practically dropping a foot of snow on them in the process.

"What the hell did I do wrong?"

Carter knew things were bad when he was talking out loud to the radio. Never had a DJ or a song or even a car commercial responded to him when he'd done that. And yet here he was in his SUV asking the radio stupid questions.

"We spent several hours giving each other pleasure. I'm sure she enjoyed it. She told me as much. So why'd she go from hot to cold in two seconds flat?"

That one was going to have to be left dangling. He didn't have time to give it much more thought. He had enough time to make it home, shower, and get to work. And one thing was for certain: when he worked, nothing, not anything, distracted him from the business at hand. He had too much riding on it, and he wouldn't let it.

Luckily the restaurant was packed all night long, so Carter didn't have time to even think about what haunted the back of his mind. Sure, he could compartmentalize with the best of them, but her words kept echoing through his head all night long.

Was he content to be only the guy for fun sex forever? Did it feel good to leave a woman like Jamie with no hope of developing a—dare he even think it—*relationship*? Was that fair to her? To remain fuck buddies, with no hope of anything more substantial, something deeper? Did he want deep?

It meant having to analyze your own wants and needs and hopes and dreams. He hated going there. He was good with helping others in his world with that, but him? No thanks. Sure, he managed and stoked his professional aspirations. But that had been enough. Or had it?

He tried to catch Jamie's attention as she was slipping out the kitchen door after closing.

"Hey," he said, running up to her.

She gave him a cursory nod.

"Hey." She kept on walking, and he tried to keep pace with her, but she was moving at a brisk clip.

"You in a hurry?"

She shook her head. "Just want to get out of here. Heading home. I'm short on sleep."

Huh. Was she taking a swipe at him? Not like they were up all night fucking. That was all day. Then again, maybe it took it out of her. But then again, maybe it was the emotional toll it had taken on her that made her feel so weary.

"Can we talk?"

She shook her head again. "I don't think we have anything to say. I'm good with that, Carter. You've made your intentions abundantly clear. I get it."

He reached for her shoulder to turn her toward him, but she brushed him off.

"Really, Carter. It's fine. I'm good. Let's leave it at that."

She clicked her key fob and opened the car door, got in, and shut it quickly behind her.

It felt symbolic, her closing the door on him like that. And for some reason, for the first time in forever, ending a relationship before it even started didn't sit well with him.

Chapter Twenty-Three

JAMIE grabbed a glass of red from a passing waiter. She was gonna need it to get through this night. She and Maddie had been working overtime getting everything set up for tonight's auction. They'd reviewed in detail every guy with even a scintilla of potential who would be auctioned off tonight, and not a one of them appealed to her. Granted, it was off-season, so there were fewer men to choose from, but still. She wasn't feeling it, which was a bummer, since the whole reason they worked the bachelor committee was to skim off the top.

"I'm sorry you and Carter didn't hit it off," Maddie said as she scrolled down the checklist on the notepad she was holding. "I thought for sure you two would get along."

Jamie shook her head. "No worries, Mad. He's not my type."

"What is your type?"

"Ones who aren't afraid of giving themselves up a little to a relationship, for a start."

Maddie turned and looked at her. "Wait a minute. You make that sound as if you and Carter had something going there."

She shook her head. "Nah. Just a little fling. Nothing

more, nothing less."

"You and Carter had a fling? Right under my nose?"

Jamie tugged on her sweater dress, which kept riding up. "Trust me, there was nothing there. Nothing whatsoever."

Maddie squinted at her. "Methinks the lady doth protest too loudly."

"Honestly, Maddie. I'm kind of over it. I wasn't looking for a quickie and Carter was. We clearly have different agendas. It's fine. Oh God, don't look now." She glanced over at her parents, who were holding hands and coming toward her.

"Mom. Dad. Uh…"

"Jamie, sweetheart," her mother said, giving her a hug.

Jamie, frowned, wiggling her finger between her parents. "This?"

"Honey, we've been meaning to tell you," her mother said, gazing with loving eyes at her husband. "We've decided to reconcile."

Jamie curled her lip as if she'd tasted something rancid. "*Reconcile?*"

"Daddy and I have had some long heart-to-heart talks, and we've decided that we want to give things another try."

Jamie squinted. "After all the bullshit that went down? After all the crap you put me through? *Now* everything is hunky-dory? You've got to be kidding me."

A waiter walked by with a tray of appetizers and she grabbed three, popping them into her mouth in quick succession. Thank God for the comfort of food, she thought, not even considering what it was she was putting into her mouth… content to stuff her emotions with something handy.

Her father held up his hands. "I know, James. We have a lot to make up to you. And I have a lot to make up to your mother. But I'm committed—we're committed—to seeing this through."

"But over the past year, you broke up our family. You sold our home. You said horrible things to each other. And you"—she pointed at her father—"you betrayed your marriage vows. You had sex with the housekeeper, who was young enough to be your daughter."

Her father frowned. "Yes, to all of that. And yes, it was my fault that this all happened. And I've regretted every stinking moment of it. To be truthful, I didn't know how to get out of the mess I'd made. So I let it snowball and get worse and worse until it seemed impossible to fix."

Her mother pulled her father closer to her. "But nothing is impossible to fix. And that's a lesson that we can all take from this, sweetheart. Your father made a huge mistake. And then compounded it with even more. He was too proud to admit how badly he'd messed up. And I was so angry, I couldn't give him any space to even get there with me. So maybe I had a hand in it as well."

"Don't you take the credit for what he did," Jamie said, glaring at her father.

"Honey, I'm not taking the credit, or the blame. I'm saying that none of us is perfect, and sometimes the best thing you can do for yourself—and for those you love most—is to learn how to forgive."

Her father leaned in and kissed her mother on the lips. This was going to take some getting used to, Jamie thought. How could people go from love to hate to love again, like they were merely crossing the street or something?

"So, now what?" Jamie said, trying to absorb this all.

"Daddy's moving in with me, and we'll rent out his place for a while. As far as the big house, well, we'd been talking about downsizing for ages anyhow, so maybe it forced our hands to do what we needed to do, to get rid of all of that baggage that you drag around with you for years."

"And the gallery?"

"To be honest, it freed me up once I got rid of it," her mother said. "Now your father and I can travel a bit, which we kept saying we wanted to do."

"Daddy owns a restaurant," she said. "He can't simply up and go away."

"But that's where you're wrong, sweetie," he said. "Once you're comfortable with things, I can leave you in charge. I know you'll do an excellent job of it."

Her? Running Red Fish Blue Fish? Did that mean she could fire the chef maybe? Or perhaps relish being in charge of him and giving him shit all the time. That might be even more fun.

This was all a lot for her to digest. She was going to have to mull it all over.

"In the meantime, honey, I hope you can be happy for us," her mother said, pulling her in for another hug. "You know how much we both regret having put you in the middle of things. It was quite selfish of us, and we hope you'll forgive us."

Stupefied, Jamie nodded. Up was down and black was white and her parents were back together and Red Fish Blue Fish was going to ultimately be her baby. She was going from homeless and aimless to having a bonded family unit and a real career, all in the span of five minutes. Weird.

She nodded. "Uh, yeah. I mean, I'd be lying if I didn't say you both did some shitty things. But I guess if you're willing to forgive, then it would be wrong of me not to also." She looked at her watch. "But I've got to get going for now—this thing is going to start soon and I have to make sure everything is set with our bachelors."

Her mother hugged her father. "Well, you can take this bachelor off the menu for good."

Jamie smiled weakly. Yeah, there was that.

Maddie came up and looped arms with Jamie. "I hope you don't mind my eavesdropping on that," she said. "I know you're having mixed emotions about it all now—and I don't blame you. But to be honest, I'm kind of jealous of you."

"Jealous?" Jamie looked at her and swirled her finger to her head, indicating she was crazy. "My parents have obviously lost their marbles and are trying to drag me down with them."

"Oh, sweetie, I can't tell you how much I'd have

loved to have had my parents get back together. It would have saved a lot of grief in my household. A shitload of misery, to be sure."

Jamie thought about that for a second. "I'm sorry. That was pretty insensitive of me, wasn't it?"

Maddie shook her head and gave her friend a hug. "Not at all. You have every right to be a bit shocked and weirded out by it all. But try to keep an open mind. I think you had to learn the hard way that your folks are human beings. And sometimes human beings do stupid things." She grabbed Jamie's hand. "Now let's go make sure all of the bachelors are checked in and ready to go. If we can't buy one for ourselves, at least we can help some other woman have a hot guy for a night."

Although Jamie knew that having a hot guy for a night was nothing when all she wanted was one for longer than the allowable time limit.

Chapter Twenty-Four

CARTER entered the room where the victims—make that bachelors—had to check in before the stupid auction. God, was he dreading this thing. What was he going to do with some strange woman who wanted to purchase his time? How weird was that? Worse still, what if no one bought him? Damn, would that be embarrassing. He hoped his bio would at least entice one hungry woman— after all, who wouldn't at the very least want a guy who could cook at their beck and call for a night? He was good with that—he could fix a veritable feast and the night would go fast then. He could even show her how to do it, make it interactive. By the time they prepped, cooked, and ate, the night would be over and he'd be off the damn hook.

Of course, who would be at check-in but none other than Jamie.

He shrugged a hello. "I don't suppose you could spare a few minutes to talk with me before this debacle?" He said it loud intentionally, hoping that would agitate her into giving him the time of day.

She hissed at him. "Keep your voice down. Don't call it that. This is an important fundraiser for a good cause."

He sighed. "Please, Jamie. Give me five minutes."

She grabbed him and marched him back behind a potted palm down the hall. "What do you want from me? Because I'm not interested if you plan to defend your preference for casual affairs. That sort of thing bores me, so if that's all you want then consider the conversation over."

"Wait a minute," he said. "I thought you were the queen of casual affairs. Weren't you the one banging two guys at once?"

She glared at him. "It wasn't at the same time. Just during the same time. There's a difference."

"Not hardly."

"Yes, hardly." She threw him the stink eye. "Besides, it's not as if I completely shunned the idea of ever having something more with either of them. I mean, they weren't that kind of relationship. Or relationships. Whatever. I was in a tricky time, feeling sad and lonely and wanting some affection. None of us were looking for anything more than what we had. We liked each other, we were sexually compatible. We had fun together. But I no sooner wanted a long-term relationship with either Nick or Toby than they did with me. They were fly-by-night surfers. We had fun on the beach. And in the bedroom. And even out to dinner, or over drinks, or playing board games even. But we weren't looking for anything more long-lasting than that. I knew they'd be moving on, and I was perfectly fine with that. I mean, sure, I'd miss the sex, but it was all good. We were all on the same page." She paused and fixed her gaze on his. "At least I'm not a coward when it comes to relationships. Unlike some people who shall remain nameless."

"I'm not a coward."

"Keep on telling yourself that little bit of fiction, Carter."

He knit his brows. "I'm not. I only know that I'm not cut out for long-term. It's not in my DNA."

"That's a crock of shit and you know it. You're afraid. And by afraid, I mean you're a coward."

"Don't tell me that. I spent most of my life filling in the gaps left behind by my parents' failed relationship. I was brave in caring for my sister, for my father. I'm the opposite of cowardly."

"Yeah, but in all of that caring, did it ever once cross your mind to care for you?"

He stood perfectly still. An announcement came over a loudspeaker, asking people to take their seats so the auction could begin.

"Look, I've got to go," Jamie said.

And for once in Carter's life, he truly didn't want a woman he liked to slip through his hands.

The ick factor had suddenly become super high for Jamie when she realized that her father had volunteered to be one of the bachelors to be auctioned off. Seriously? As if.

Turns out it was a ruse, and he was put up there by

her mother to give them a chance to make a fairly public statement to anyone in town that they were back together again. Jamie had to give it to her mom—at least it went for a good cause. She cringed at the idea that any woman would actually bid on her father for a night, and Lord knows what her intentions with him would be, but it never came to that. Her mom had asked her friend Cynthia McCreary to counterbid her to add some excitement and ratchet up the donation.

Drinks had been flowing freely—with the idea that the drunker the audience got, the higher the bids would be. And judging by the level of shouting out bids and the squeals of delight from the winners each time, it was working.

Jamie was sitting next to Maddie at a table toward the back of the hotel room, glancing down at the program, counting down how many more men till she could go home and get to bed. She was bored, she was tired, and she was cranky. Oh and she was "hangry," that cursed condition of being hungry while pissed. There weren't nearly enough hors d'oeuvres to go around—part of the 'get 'em drunk' strategy—and so she'd barely had anything to eat. Oddly enough her diet and fitness routine had been working, and she was down a dress size since January first. It didn't help that she'd been mooning over the idiot chef. Plus maybe the added sex boosted her metabolism. Not that they'd had that much sex yet, but still. Perhaps the wishful thinking had contributed.

"Oooh, ladies. Next up we have Carter, who knows that a way to a woman's heart is through her stomach," the announcer said as the audience oohed and aahed at the mere idea of having some man who could cook at your command. Jamie rolled her eyes because yeah, he was a helluva chef and knew his way around a kitchen—not to mention around a woman's body—and, well, what he did with that dessert clearly showed he knew how to combine the two. But a hell of a lot of help that was when all he planned was a wham-bam-thank-you-ma'am and then on to the next woman.

"Let's start the bidding at twenty-five. Do I hear twenty-five?"

Jamie looked up and saw a hand go up toward the front. She couldn't tell who it was but wished her good luck with the man.

"Do I hear fifty? Anyone?"

Another hand went up, over to her left. It looked like her dental hygienist. How weird would that be, knowing they'd both slept with the same man. Except ugh, that thought was annoying as hell. Why would he want to sleep with someone else when he made it abundantly clear he enjoyed sleeping with her? Then again, guys never thought twice about sticking that thing wherever the wind blew.

"How about a hundred?" the auctioneer continued. Ladies? Imagine how good he must be with his hands, considering what he does for a living."

Three hands went up, including Olivia's, the hostess from work, darn her, which must've made the auctioneer cocky because the bidding jumped at that point.

"Do we have two hundred for the chef with the talented hands?"

Three tables over, a super drunk woman holding a paddle shot her arm up and shouted at the top of her lungs, "Three hundred!" A cheer went up at her table, with everyone patting her on the back. That's when Jamie noticed it was the WVBH-TV table, and the bidder was none other than the wretched Jennifer Lorenzini. If that didn't hit below the belt, nothing did.

"Four hundred!" That one was super close by. Jamie looked around and she saw Maddie had raised her paddle and called out the bid. What the fuck?

"Five fifty!" Jennifer Lorenzini the twat screamed out. She wasn't even waiting for the auctioneer to suggest a number. She was spewing out bids in a desperate attempt to bed Carter Henderson, the bitch.

"Seven hundred!" Jamie looked at Maddie as if she'd grown horns and a spiked tail. She leaned over and whispered behind her hand into her ear. "What the fuck are you doing?"

Maddie waved her away.

"Nine hundred and fifty!" came the sloshed voice of that shitshow of a news reporter. Jamie had half a mind to slug her. She was so desperate for a guy she'd pay a thousand bucks for him? What a bitch. Jamie chose to ignore the fact that if it was any other woman bidding on some other guy she'd have been heartened about their philanthropic intentions to help those poor abused women. So what if she was hypocritical. It was her prerogative as a quasi-jilted woman. Nevertheless, she made a mental note to consider doing a little soul-searching come morning. But right now, she was pissed.

"Two thousand, five hundred!" The crowd hushed, and all eyes turned toward their table. Only the woman holding the paddle wasn't Maddie but was instead none other than a very jealous Jamie Lundquist, who was damned if she was going to let fucking Jennifer Lorenzini get naked with her man. A very jealous Jamie Lundquist who felt the hot rush of embarrassment—no, make that complete and utter mortification—as her face no doubt turned a rather unbecoming crimson hue. Before she knew it, she'd covered her mouth with her hand, the auctioneer was closing out the bidding, and all she could hear was "sold, to the woman in the sweater dress for two thousand, five hundred dollars."

Chapter Twenty-Five

CARTER could not believe how embarrassing it was to stand up on the makeshift stage in surfer shorts and no top—his sister made him dress that way—while drunken women shamelessly cackled at him or at the women who were willing to pay for him or whatever it was they were yucking it up about. He wanted nothing more than to crawl under a rock and hide from the world. Not only for this but also for what a complete ass he'd been with Jamie.

Sadly it was too little too late for him now, he realized. Because it took him till now to understand that the feelings he had for Jamie weren't the usual ones easily sated with a roll in the hay. At last, it had dawned on him that Jamie was the first woman he wanted to learn how to be with. Granted it sounded weird that he would have to learn that, but he did. He'd gone along with the notion of having one-dimensional affairs and nothing more. But Jamie made him want to be a better man, made him want to prove to her that he could be in a relationship with her.

Yet the look she gave him shortly before his stint on stage told him in no uncertain terms that she'd rather lop off his balls with a Chinese cleaver. He'd had plenty of experience prepping food with one of those babies, so he knew how wicked bad that would be.

He looked out over the audience, and it was hard to discern who was who with the bright lights beaming on him. It's a good thing he'd been working out the past few months at least—his pecs were looking decent, his legs were strong, he'd whittled away some of that residual holiday gut that showed up every year in December. At least he wasn't thoroughly embarrassing himself.

He heard some ridiculous bid and strained to see who on earth would make that. Ugh, it was that handsy TV reporter who seemed bent on winning Carter for the night. He hesitated to imagine what an evening with her might entail. She gave off a vibe that she would have him tied to the bed with a ball gag in his mouth and a crop on his ass in no time flat, with her in a rubber corset and six-inch stilettos. He'd made a deal with his sister, which was going to be his saving grace here. He told her if anyone too awful started bidding on him, she was to outbid the woman, and Carter would pay her back. Not that he was Mr. Moneybags, but he'd figure out a way to shell out a few hundred bucks, tops.

Sure enough, Maddie started counterbidding, but the drunken reporter kept jacking up her bid. What the hell?

Then other women were following suit: mob mentality at its finest. This was getting out of hand. He about died when the reporter bid almost a thousand bucks. He'd told Maddie not to exceed that amount. What the hell was he going to do with her for a night? He was going to need a bodyguard to protect him.

And then he heard the voice, clear as a bell. Two thousand, five hundred dollars. From none other than

Jamie, the woman who hated his guts. Now the question was whether she planned to use her free night with him to slowly torture him to death. Or did she have something more mutually agreeable in mind?

"Whoa, dude, what was *that* all about?" Maddie had turned to her friend, shaking her head. "In a million years, I couldn't have predicted that outcome."

Jamie felt numb. From the tips of her toes to the hair on her head, everything seemed frozen and motionless and completely devoid of any ability to feel. Maybe even think.

"What the hell possessed you to bid that much money on my brother? I thought you didn't even like him!"

Jamie opened her mouth to speak, but nothing came out. People had gathered around to congratulate her, but she didn't know what to say. Shouldn't they be expressing their sympathy instead? As in, "I'm sorry, Jamie, you spent the bulk of your savings on a guy you have no chance with."

She was still processing the whole thing, trying to figure out how she'd made such a colossal mistake, when the crowd around her parted, and there before her stood Carter, in his board shorts and no shirt, and frankly he looked delectable. She was afraid to look into his eyes, so instead she stared at that cut V of his abdomen. She loved that on a man. And that led her eyes to the happy trail of hair that disappeared beneath the waistband of his swimsuit, and she sure as hell knew where that led her: Valhalla. The promised land. His big, amazing cock. She wasn't sure, but she might have licked her lips... in case she hadn't embarrassed herself enough.

"Jamie?" he said, breaking her from her reverie as he waved his hands in front of her eyes.

She shook her head to clear her thinking and looked hard into his face.

"I'd have seriously stopped at like fifty bucks," he said as he reached for her hand. She merely nodded as he pulled her along and led her away from the crowd through an exit door and down a back hallway. They entered a small sitting room with a sofa and TV. It was tuned to some reality show about a morbidly obese woman trying to go on about her business in a fat-averse world.

He nodded at the television. "I can't imagine it's particularly good for your heart to be carrying around that much weight," he said. "But I applaud her decision to tell the rest of the world to fuck off if she's fine with being the way she is."

Jamie nodded, still overwhelmed by the course of events.

"The truth is, I always like a little meat on my women," he said. "Not that you have a lot of meat on you. In fact looks to me like you've lost weight since our first shitty encounter." He peered around to look at her ass. "But your ass, shit, I can't begin to explain its perfection exactly the way it is."

"Are you trying to tell me something, Carter?"

He nodded, pulling her toward him and settling them both on the sofa. "In my own stupid, ham-handed way, I am." He scooched her dress up so that he could lift one of her legs over his and she could straddle him. His hard length pressed against her, with nothing but her underwear and his shorts between them. It took her breath away. Their faces were mere inches apart. Carter placed his pointer finger beneath her chin and softly pulled her toward him. "I love the feeling of your body pressed against mine, Jamie Lundquist."

She nodded.

"And I love the anticipation of knowing your lips are about to settle over mine. That our tongues will soon be tangling, straining toward one another in a sensual dance that is but one step in where we're headed."

He placed a soft kiss on her lips, then continued. "I love that I get excited thinking about you. Wondering what you're doing. Wondering if you're as excited about me as I am about you."

He stroked his fingers through her hair, then pressed his forehead to hers, breathing softly against her.

"I love that my mind races trying to come up with new and inventive ways that I can pleasure you." He frowned. "And I hated the idea that I might never have that chance again."

She thrust out her lower lip in a pout and he caught it between his teeth.

"I love that you dumped your coffee on me when I was such an asshole to you. I love that you didn't keep your anger to yourself, but you made me know you were pissed at me."

"You deserved it," she said softly.

"Ahhh… she speaks."

She nodded.

"I love that for the first time in my life I know that I'm ready to have a grown-up relationship with a woman I've fallen head over heels for, despite myself."

A smile started to spread across Jamie's face.

"And I hate that I might have ruined my chances with someone who seems to have taken on a larger-than-life importance in my world." His green eyes fixed on her brown ones. "Could you find it in your heart to give me another chance?"

She slowly started to nod, as he slipped a hand under her dress and his fingers found their way to the lower edge of her panties. He moved a finger under them, where she was wet, a dead giveaway if ever there was one. He slid his finger through her folds before inserting it inside of her, then used his thumb to stimulate her clit. Jamie's breathing became labored as he continued to play with her; then his other hand massaged her breast through her dress and the thin layer of her bra, pinching her nipple hard till she moaned loudly.

"Where are we?" she said. "Is someone going to walk in on us in here?"

He shook his head. "We're good. It was the 'green room' for tonight's talent. Since the auction is over, I suspect we've got the place to ourselves."

She nodded. "Oh, so you're clever, are you?"

He inserted another finger inside of her, curving them toward her pelvis and hitting the right spot, and she thrust hard into his hand. His mouth traveled across her jawline, placing kisses along the way.

"Not to mention talented, if your body's response to my ministrations is any indication."

"I can hardly disagree with you on that," she said, moving her hips faster against his talented fingers until she felt the familiar stirrings deep in her pelvis. When Carter bit down on her nipple through her dress, she lost it, her hips grinding against his hand, her pussy convulsing around his fingers as stars shot across her line of vision, and her pelvis shuddered in spasms.

It took a minute for her breathing to settle down before Carter asked her another question.

"Do you mind my asking?"

She lifted a brow. "Asking what?"

"Why? Why would you pay that kind of money for me? I was nothing but a disappointment to you."

She wrapped her arms around him, pressing herself against his hard cock again.

"I suppose because sometimes fate needs a little extra shove."

She didn't bother mentioning she wasn't about to let her nemesis have a chance at happiness with the man she already knew she could find her own joy with. She could save that for another day.

"So you saw through me, did you?"

She nodded. "You were transparent enough." She smooshed her mouth to the side in thought. "Well, enough that I impulsively decided to try once more to convince you."

"So what are your plans for me now that you practically own me?"

She started to slide her hand down the front of his shorts. "First I'm going to have my wicked way with you," she said as she loosened the Velcro of his suit to ease her access. "And then we'll talk about other creative uses for my slave for a day."

"Might I suggest playing with our food again?"

Jamie wrapped her fingers around his cock and stroked him up and down.

"Most definitely. With one provision."

He lifted a brow. "Oh, yeah."

"Nothing involving a pork chop."

They both laughed.

"Mark my words—I promise if I ever call you 'pork chop' again, it's only because it's a term of endearment, okay?"

"Deal." She grinned. "Now give me that cock of mine," she said, "because it is mine now."

"All of me is yours now, Jamie."

"And don't you forget it. Now shut up and show me what you can do with that thing." She slid herself onto his swollen cock, happy to know this would be the first of many times with the man who was finally able to give himself, heart and soul, to her.

Thank you so much for reading **Falling for Mr. Sometimes**! I hope you enjoyed it! If so, please help others find this book:

1. Help other people find this book by writing a review.

2. Sign up for my new releases email so you can find out about the next book as soon as it's available and get fun giveaways.
   http://eepurl.com/baaewn

3. Like my Facebook page.
   www.facebook.com/jennygardinerbooks

And I love to hear from readers! Let me know what you think about my books! You can write to me at jenny@jennygardiner.net, and visit me on the web at www.jennygardiner.net.

Keep reading for a sample from **Falling for Mr. Right**, the next book in the Falling for Mr. Wrong series.

Falling

for

Mr. Right

by Jenny Gardiner

Chapter One

SOMETIMES before a big competition, Madison Henderson felt like a boxer prepping for a showdown match: obsessively adhering to pre-"fight" rituals so that everything worked in her favor. First she put on her noise-cancelling Bose headphones—the ones that cost about as much as a small car—so she could tune out any and all distractions. She had her phone loaded with super zen music—the kind you'd hear at a spa or when you got acupuncture treatment: a lot of rainwater and seabirds and waves crashing on the shoreline and native American flutes—and she closed her eyes while absorbing the peaceful sounds. Anything to sooth her jangled nerves.

Then she visualized what victory looked like for her: how she'd win and how the audience would react to her win.

She wished she could wrap herself in a satin boxer's robe and have a trainer massage her shoulders, which she knew would be about as tight as a virgin's snatch by the time the night was out. Except she didn't have a trainer, so never mind that luxury. It was true when she got anxious she scrunched her shoulders up toward her ears and always paid for it the next day with a sore neck and shoulders. Assuming she won tonight, she'd spring for a masseuse with some of the winnings to take care of that problem.

Next came the mindful self-affirmations she went over in her mind:

I am the architect of my life; I built its foundation and choose its contents.

Today, I am brimming with energy and overflowing with joy.

I am superior to negative thoughts and low actions.

I have been given endless talents, which I begin to utilize today.

I possess the qualities needed to be extremely successful.

Creative energy surges through me and leads me to new and brilliant ideas.

My ability to conquer my challenges is limitless; my potential to succeed is infinite.

I am at peace with all that has happened, is happening and will happen.

I'm the fucking queen of trivia.

Well, that last one wasn't necessarily as mindful a thought as the other ones, but she knew it was true, and sometimes a little excessive confidence was in order.

It was a good thing she wasn't like a baseball player, or she'd swear off shaving her legs or changing her underwear or sex until she lost a match. And by now she'd have some serious gorilla legs because she hadn't lost in a long time. Not to mention dirty underwear. Though thanks, but no thanks—so not her style. Maddie preferred her panties to be the super girlie girl kind, and definitely clean. As far as the sex thing, well, the bummer was life had sort of defaulted into sex-free anyhow, considering the dearth of relationships she'd been mired in for far too long, so that was a moot point. But were it a factor in her life, no way would she put an end to that just to win a game.

But was trivial night just a game? Not so much for Maddie. It was kind of her thing, so she had a lot invested in it. And for that reason, yeah, she got super nervous before a match (okay, so nobody else called them matches but her. She recognized that was a little hyper competitive). She reminded herself regularly that her pre-competition jitters were normal—what anyone would experience before a big sparring event.

This all could seem a bit dramatic for someone bracing to compete in her local bar's trivia night. It wasn't as if she was prepping to win the Boston Marathon. Or to drill into someone's brain for delicate neurosurgery. But nevertheless, she was a big believe in being prepared, and showing up as the best "you" you could be. Besides, she freaking loved to win. Loved it. And dammit she could, too: no one stored more useless trivial knowledge in her brains than she did. Blame it on DNA, maybe. Or perhaps the fault rested at the feet of her first serious relationship, with a boy two years her senior and the once-love her life. The one that got away. Ish. More like the one she'd love to push out a second story window if she ever saw his miserable ratfink ass again, after the way he ditched her without a backward glance.

Ugh, stirring up negative thoughts about that traitor Donovan Reeves did nothing to help settle her anxiety. Maddie felt keyed up, jittery, like she'd had three cups of espresso and an IV infusion of Terbutaline. But she needed to focus, re-direct her mind to the business at hand. Yet now that Donovan had reared his unwelcome self into her psyche, her brain kept straying back to thoughts of him, unbidden—to the times they challenged each other to stupid contests over mindless factoids. The year their high school quiz team won the state championships. The hours they spent pouring through Trivia Pursuit cards, throwing down the gauntlet to one another to see who would choke first.

For them it was all about the challenge, not really the knowledge. If you could call it knowledge. Challenge? Who was she kidding? It was more like foreplay, some bizarre libido-enhancing ritual that got them crazy hot and bothered. Or maybe they were already hot and bothered, and they just liked to play trivia quizzes. But somehow they seemed to do that all the time—the trivia games. Oh, and the sexual games as well.

Sometimes they'd even throw down a trivia challenge to decide who got to do what to the other. Hmmm. Maybe they were just weird. Oddballs, yet perfect for one another. At least that's what Maddie thought, until stupid Donovan up and bailed on her just as he was leaving for college, when she thought they were going to continue dating indefinitely, and instead he just cut off communications and left town.

Having had a mother who'd walked out on her and her brother Carter when they were younger meant that the only reason Maddie would ever want to see Donovan's face again would be to slug it for betraying her so cruelly, particularly under the circumstances, and leaving her heart in tatters. But Donovan hadn't been back to Verity Beach in forever—she heard through the grapevine he was a doctor now, not that she'd asked around. She was just glad it was somewhere far away, from what she recalled. So island in the Pacific, or some nation at war. It didn't matter to her, as long as she'd never have to encounter that miserable face of his ever again. Even if he did have a pair of sexy brown eyes that sucked you in and made you feel all warm and cozy and safe. As if. At least now she knew what lying eyes those were all along.

She really had to get him out of her head or thoughts of that would psyche her totally out, and she needed to win tonight. She was determined to crush the competition in the statewide trivia championships, so working the local weekly games at pubs in the Verity Beach area to train would keep her sharp and ready for the looming competition for which she'd qualified.

Maddie took a deep breath, in through her nose, and exhaled through her mouth, releasing all the tension that had been building up. She repeated it a few more times. She could do this. She flipped down her car visor, switched on the lighted mirror, then spread on a little more lipstick and one more layer of mascara to highlight her seaglass-green eyes, pulled off the ponytail holder that had been containing a mass of curly dark hair, which she gave a strong shake to, then reached for her car keys and turned off the ignition, grabbed her purse, and exited the car. As she approached the massive twenty-foot three-dimensional hook-legged pirate that stood sentry atop the roof of the Peg Leg, she gave a nod to the veritable patron saint of this dark, crusty old pub that had been in Verity Beach for as long as Maddie could remember.

She grabbed the (somewhat tasteless) pirate hook door handle and entered the bar. As her eyes adjusted to the dim light inside the low-ceilinged space, she recognized her small team already seated at a table near the emcee stand that was set up in the center of the room. She glanced at the list of team names that had been posted for the night's competition, noticing the usual suspects: Don't Know Much About History (she always beat them handily), Just the Facts Ma'am (those guys couldn't win a competition if their lives depended on it), then her team, Trivia Newton John, high scorers extraordinaire, natch. Then she noticed another team she'd not heard of before: Tequila Mockingbird. Huh. She wondered who headed up that group. She thought she knew all the trivia groups in town.

She greeted her trivia team: Olivia Singletary, who was a hostess at Red Fish Blue Fish, where her brother was head chef; Tamara Thompson, who managed a small bed and breakfast in town; and Jesse Montgomery who did some sort of IT work that Maddie didn't even pretend to understand.

They high-fived each other and Olivia handed Maddie her usual beer—a pint draft of a local IPA, which she drank at every trivia night, just to keep things the same for good measure. Not that she was superstitious, but still.

"Hey so who is this new group I see posted?" Maddie said, taking a sip of her beer.

Tamara shrugged. "Tequila something or other. I have no idea. Don't recognize them." She pointed toward a guy in a blue and white ticking button-down and khaki shorts whose back was to them.

"Weird. So unexpected to have newbies out of nowhere show up like that. Usually you hear something at least through the grapevine."

The emcee, Joey Farmiggio, announced the game was about to begin, so players settled into their seats, their pens at the ready.

This was when Maddie always made sure to aim a strategically placed cold hard stare into the eyes of her adversaries, hoping to intimidate them just a little bit, before they had a chance to do so to her.

Maddie turned to glance at team Tequila Mockingbird, thinking it would be best to cast her steely-eyed glare their way first, only to have her eyes meet a pair of brown ones that made her gasp.

Because there before her was the very man she hoped never to see again, the one she fantasized about punching in the face for years, the one who shat all over her happiness like he was a pigeon and she a random car parked beneath his roosting tail.

And he had the audacity to break out into a huge grin.

What a miserable rat bastard.

Chapter Two

DONOVAN Reeves had made some good decisions in his life and some bad ones. And he'd learned through some of his better decisions that you ultimately needed to accept what you've done and move on—life could be brutal, so you do what you can, fix what you screwed up, if possible, and don't beat yourself up too badly over any of it.

He'd just returned to his hometown of Verity Beach, in the Outer Banks of North Carolina, after many years away, first in college, then in medical school, then his residency in emergency medicine, and finally a stint in the Democratic Republic of the Congo, the DRC, as a doctor with Médicins Sans Frontières, known as MSF, or Doctors without Borders.

For years he'd felt a restlessness in him that he couldn't quite quench, so he'd volunteered with MSF, hoping it would quell whatever unease kept him feeling on edge so much. During his many years of medical training, he figured it had more to do with lack of sleep, plus being keyed up from the constant need to learn, study, prepare, and perform. He'd hoped immersing himself into a different culture with people whose needs far exceeded his own—or those he could ever even fathom—would disarm his anxiousness. Maybe reducing life to its most base level would lower the intensity of his disquietude.

And boy, was he right. Working often seven days a week for months on end with the most rudimentary of medical equipment and supplies, with people whose ailments and suffering and degrees of malnutrition were so very unfamiliar to him, certainly took the onus away from him. He barely had time to brush his teeth, let alone wonder or worry what had once kept him up at night or mentally pacing the floors by day.

Of course the flip side of that was nearly a year working under pretty primitive medical conditions with children dying on his watch from the most preventable of diseases like measles and cholera had left him burned out and in need of a change of scenery. Before his stint in the Congo, he'd ben seeking the unknown, and he found it in a big way. He'd toiled under harsh conditions a world away from the comfortable life he'd always known. He was very proud of the work he'd accomplished, and hoped he'd made at least a small difference in the lives of the people he'd met in the DRC. But his brain and his body were fried and he truly needed something to revitalize his spirit. He'd hoped some of his mom's home-cooking and the familiarity of a life he once knew would help to restore some balance in his life.

So here he was, back home, wondering if what he really needed was what he'd known all along: the comforts of home, family and friends: the very thing he walked way from years earlier in an effort to spread his wings a bit and try on a new life, one not under the thumb of his demanding father.

He'd only been back in town for a week, after his debriefing with MSF in Paris. Wow, was that weird, going from the primitive world of the DRC—where the daily effort of life was exhausting, be it ensuring you have potable water, or navigating your way on a motorcycle through dubious roads washed away into three-foot deep mud pits by rainy seasons deluges—to the bright lights of Paris and the abundance that went along with that.

Nothing comes easy for those living in countries like the DRC—the needs are so great, the availability so minimal; life is a perpetual hardship and aspirations are so low on the one hand, but the tolerance of such struggles so impressively high. Donovan figured if you don't have the expectation for things to get better, eventually you accept what you have and learn to live with is as best you can. For the people he grew to love while living there, this was of course all they ever knew, so despite dire living conditions, each day they greeted him with a smile and kind words. It taught him much about how best to live a life.

Which brought him back to why he was sitting in this dingy bar, gearing up for a game of trivia that felt, frankly, incredibly trivial after all he'd been through this past year. But he'd be lying to himself if he didn't admit the true reason he'd come back to Verity Beach: he'd hoped to make amends with his childhood sweetheart, a girl he'd loved deeply but whose heart be broke for her own good more than a decade ago. He'd hated to do it, but he knew (or thought he knew) he'd made the right choice—egged on by his domineering father, who had put such pressure on Donovan to follow in his footsteps and who'd pressed him to cut all ties before leaving Verity Beach. What was an obedient son to do but listen to his father?

Donovan had done a little forensics work upon his return home, got the low-down on Maddie Henderson's life, learned with great relief there was no man occupying a spot in it, and mapped out a way to at least try to ingratiate himself back into her world. That is, if she didn't beat him up, or bludgeon him to death, or maybe grab that gigantic pirate's cutlass on the wall over there and stab him in the heart. Because the truth of the matter was, she had every right to. And if he was Maddie, there's no way he'd even speak to him, let alone reconcile. So he could hardly blame her if she refused to look at him, let alone speak to him.

But a man could hope. And one thing that Donovan learned over the past year is that human beings could live through a lot with a little bit of hope.

"What the ever-loving fuck are you doing here?" He heard that voice that instantly quieted the entire bar, and something inside of him ached at the sound of it.

But then his head registered precisely what she said, and his heart sank just a bit.

It seemed maybe hope was an overrated emotion after all.

Falling for Mr. Right
Coming July 17, 2018

About the Author

Jenny Gardiner is the author of #1 Kindle Bestseller *Slim to None* and the award-winning novel *Sleeping with Ward Cleaver*. Her latest works are the *It's Reigning Men* series, the *Royal Romeos* series and her new *Falling for Mr. Wrong* series. She also published the memoir *Winging It: A Memoir of Caring for a Vengeful Parrot Who's Determined to Kill Me,* now re-titled *Bite Me: a Parrot, a Family and a Whole Lot of Flesh Wounds*; the novels *Anywhere but Here*; *Where the Heart Is*; the essay collection *Naked Man on Main Street*, and *Accidentally on Purpose* and *Compromising Positions* (writing as Erin Delany); and is a contributor to the humorous dog anthology *I'm Not the Biggest Bitch in This Relationship*.

Her work has been found in Ladies Home Journal, the Washington Post, Marie-Claire.com, and on NPR's Day to Day. She was also a columnist for Charlottesville's Daily Progress for over a decade, and is the Volunteer Coordinator for the Virginia Film Festival.

She has worked as a professional photographer, an orthodontic assistant (learning quite readily that she was not cut out for a career in polyester), a waitress (probably her highest-paying job), a TV reporter, a pre-obituary writer, as well as a publicist to a United States Senator (where she first learned to write fiction). She's photographed Prince Charles (and her assistant husband got him to chuckle!), Elizabeth Taylor, and the president of

164

Uganda. She and her family and menagerie of pets now live a less exotic life in Virginia.

Visit Jenny at her website at www.jennygardiner.net where you can sign up for her newsletter, visit her blog, or find her on Facebook and Twitter. And every blue moon she'll post adorable pictures of her pets on Instagram as @thejennygardiner.